Hannah was so overwhelmed by everything that before she could stop herself, she leaned up and kissed Chase on the cheek— just when he turned his head to her.

Her lips landed on his.

But instead of pulling back for all the reasons that had whizzed through her head five minutes ago, she leaned in.

So did Chase.

His lips were equally firm and soft. Mmm. She could stay here forever...

The timer went off and they both took a step back.

"That was unexpected," he said, searching her eyes.

"An accident." She rushed to speak. "I went to kiss you on the cheek and you turned at that exact moment, so neither of us meant to *kiss-kiss* each other."

"Except we both did kiss-kiss each other," he pointed out, his gaze on hers. "After the accidental collision of lips."

She stared at him, unable to look away, goose bumps trailing up her spine.

He smiled that smile, and all she wanted was to fling herself into his arms for another hug.

Another kiss.

But he was giving her a nice out and she had to take it.

Because falling for Chase Dawson was not an option.

Dear Reader,

When ranch foreman Chase Dawson arrives in a small Wyoming town to follow a lead about the father he knows nothing about, everyone seems to hate Chase. He's mistaken for someone else, someone who looks just like him.

Yet as single mother Hannah Calhoun confronts him—she thinks he's the no-good runaway father of her baby!—he realizes that he just might have an identical twin he never knew existed. About to uncover his family history, Chase needs Hannah's help...

I hope you enjoy Chase and Hannah's love story. I love to hear from readers, so feel free to email me with your thoughts about *The Cowboy's Mistaken Identity*. You can find more information about me and my books at my website: melissasenate.com.

Warmest regards,

Melissa Senate

The Cowboy's Mistaken Identity

MELISSA SENATE

Recycling programs
for this product may
not exist in your area.

ISBN-13: 978-1-335-72445-8

The Cowboy's Mistaken Identity

Copyright © 2023 by Melissa Senate

For questions and comments about the quality of this book, please contact us at CustomerService@Harlequin.com.

Harlequin Enterprises ULC
22 Adelaide St. West, 41st Floor
Toronto, Ontario M5H 4E3, Canada
www.Harlequin.com

Printed in U.S.A.

Melissa Senate has written many novels for Harlequin and other publishers, including her debut, *See Jane Date*, which was made into a TV movie. She also wrote seven books for Harlequin Special Edition under the pen name Meg Maxwell. Her novels have been published in over twenty-five countries. Melissa lives on the coast of Maine with her teenage son; their rescue shepherd mix, Flash; and a lap cat named Cleo. For more information, please visit her website, melissasenate.com.

Books by Melissa Senate

Harlequin Special Edition

Dawson Family Ranch

Wyoming Matchmaker
His Baby No Matter What
Heir to the Ranch
Santa's Twin Surprise

Furever Yours

A New Leash on Love
Home is Where the Hound Is

Montana Mavericks: The Lonelyhearts Ranch

The Maverick's Baby-in-Waiting

Montana Mavericks: The Real Cowboys of Bronco Heights

The Most Eligible Cowboy

Montana Mavericks: Brothers & Broncos

One Night with the Maverick

Visit the Author Profile page
at Harlequin.com for more titles.

For my mother

Chapter One

"You have some nerve showing your face in this town."

Chase Dawson was about to head into Mae's Diner when a man leaving the restaurant jabbed a finger at his chest.

The woman with the guy glared at Chase. "He's not worth it," she ground out. Then, as the couple pushed past him and headed down Main Street, she turned and added, "You're a despicable excuse for a human being!"

Whoa. Chase was sure glad he wasn't the man these two thought he was. Though at six foot three, with black hair, blue eyes and a cleft in his chin, he couldn't remember ever being mistaken for someone else.

He pulled open the door to the diner, anticipating a juicy cheeseburger, fries in gravy and a tall glass of sweet iced tea. He'd been on the road for five hours and had finally arrived in Winston, Wyoming, from his home in the eastern part of the state. He'd been reluctant enough to come here and finally dig into his family history, and this was the crazy welcome he got? *Doesn't bode well*, he thought.

"Well, well, look who's back in town," another female voice said, a combination of anger and sadness in her tone. "Of course, I'm not surprised that you didn't contact me."

He let go of the door and turned around. A petite blonde woman with two hands on a baby stroller stood about a foot away. She looked even madder than the couple had.

She shook her head. "Do you even care that you have a son?" she asked, her hazel-green eyes going to the stroller for a moment before shooting back to him. "A three-month-old beautiful baby boy? No, you don't. You made that clear."

Whoa again. What the heck? He'd never stepped foot in Winston, Wyoming, before two minutes ago. He'd never even been within three hours of the place. He most definitely did not have a three-month-old son.

"Ma'am, I'm sorry, but you have me mistaken for someone else," Chase said, taking off his hat so she could better see his face.

"Yeah, you're real easy to mistake," she said with an angry roll of her eyes. "Now you're pretending to be someone else? Classic gaslighting. What a piece of work you are." With that she wheeled the stroller past him down the sidewalk.

Okay, what was going on here? Could he look so much like someone else in this town that a woman thought he was the *father of her baby*?

He hurried after her, taking his wallet from his back pocket and getting out his driver's license. "Here," he said. "This will prove I'm not you who have me confused with."

She stopped and turned around. "Oh, I'm the confused one? And I don't need to see your fake license. I'm sure you have dozens of them with all kinds of aliases. Don't insult my intelligence."

"Miss. Ma'am," he said. "If you'll just listen—"

"Miss? Ma'am?" A burst of angry laughter came out of her pink-red mouth. "You know, you probably *have* forgotten my name. Well, it's Hannah Calhoun. I suppose you don't remember whispering it in my ear when you sweet-talked me into bed that first night."

"Trust me, ma'am. Hannah. I would not forget that." Had that just stupidly come out of his mouth? He shook his head. "Please—I'm not whoever you think I am. My name is Chase Dawson," he added, holding up his license, which she refused to even glance at. He put it back in his wallet. "I'm from Bear Ridge, Wyoming, five hours southeast. I've never been to Winston before but I'm here to follow up a lead on my father, who I never met and don't know a thing about. It's possible he could be from here. Could I look so much like him that I'm being mistaken for him? He'd be around twenty years older, though."

She opened her mouth to say something, but just then, two elderly men in Stetsons and cowboy boots emerged from the diner, looked his way and shook their fists at him before getting into a pickup. "Dirtbag!" one of them shouted out the window at him.

Chase was stunned into silence for a moment, staring at the truck and wondering how his first five minutes in Winston had derailed like this. He looked back at Hannah Calhoun. "I'm telling you the truth."

She narrowed her eyes. "Oh yeah? What's your father's name?"

"As I said, I don't know a thing about him—including his name."

She raised an eyebrow. "You don't know who your father is?"

"No. That's why I'm here. To solve a family mystery. I was raised by a single mother who wouldn't tell me anything about my dad. She passed away a couple months ago, and I found a piece of scrap paper among her things with *Winston, WY*, written on it and underlined. I thought maybe there was a connection to her past so I'm here to follow it. And from the way I've been greeted, I'm clearly onto something."

She tilted her head to the left and studied him, then to the right. "You swear on a stack of Bibles that you're telling the truth?"

He held his hat to his chest and looked right into her eyes. "Yes."

"Huh," she said, her expression softening for a second. Then it turned stony again. "That was Kent McCord's signature look—false sincerity. He had it mastered."

"Kent McCord?" Chase repeated. "That's the guy I look so much like?"

"So alike you could be identical twins," she said, staring at him. Studying him. Suddenly her eyes got a little misty and she shook her head. "I'm actually standing here believing your lies again. What is wrong with me? Haven't I learned you're a lying, cheating bastard who'll say anything, even the most outrageous nonsense and get people to believe it?" She glanced into the stroller, where he could see a sleeping infant with wispy dark hair peeking out from under his bear-ears fleece hat. "Just stay away from me, Kent."

With that, she turned and walked away, pushing the stroller with slumped shoulders.

He ran after her. "I'm Chase Dawson. Not Kent McCord. I don't even have a brother and certainly not an identical twin. Apparently, I have a look-alike, though."

She stopped and turned around, reaching into the tote bag snapped onto the stroller handles and pulling out a cell phone. She scrolled through photos, letting out an impatient sigh. "Here," she said, holding up the phone. "Here you are."

Chase took the phone and stared at the photo of…himself. Down to the blue eyes, the nose, the strong jawline, the cleft in the chin, the thick black hair. This was his face. And from the way the man stood very tall against a shiny black pickup, he appeared to be over six feet, like Chase.

"He looks exactly like me," Chase said. "I'll grant you that. But he has a scar by the side of his left eye. I don't." He held out the phone to her.

She took it and stared. "Huh. You're right," she said, looking from the photo to the left side of Chase's face. "But you could have had plastic surgery. I'm surprised you didn't alter your appearance more, actually, with so many people out for your blood."

Jeez. Just what had this man done to earn the wrath of so many? "I don't know how else to prove to you that I'm not who you think I am."

She leaned in a bit, studying him again—hard. "You know, now that I look more closely, really closely, there's something slightly different about the shape and intensity of your eyes. Kent's eyes were just a bit softer somehow. Helped him get his way."

A small bit of relief hit him in the chest. Helped *him* get his way meant she was starting to believe he wasn't this Kent McCord. A man Chase clearly didn't want to be.

A car coming down Main Street slowed, and a teenager in the passenger seat threw something right at him. It landed on his thigh and bounced to the ground by his foot. Chase looked down. A wadded-up fast food wrapper from Quik Burger. "Jerk!" the kid called out as the car kept going.

Chase threw his arms up in the air. Even teenagers hated him. "I came here for answers about my past," he said. "But it sure looks like no one is going to talk to me, anyway. Everyone thinks I'm this really bad dude."

Her head tilted again, and then she let out a

breath. She studied him harder, peering closely at his face. She let out another impatient sigh. "There's a park up ahead with a coffee truck. I could use a cup and a rest on one of the benches. We can talk there while Danny sleeps."

She started pushing the stroller and he followed, putting his hat back on and pulling it down *way* low.

Hannah Calhoun turned the stroller into the entrance to the park, glad "Chase Dawson" hadn't said a word during the two block walk. She still didn't know what to think. She'd been up close and very personal with Kent McCord for two months. The guy beside her, with the exact physique and voice and face, save the small scar near his left eye, was a dead ringer.

Jolting to the say the least.

Despite the bright sunshine, it was still chilly this mid-April late afternoon, so the park was thankfully close to empty. The last thing she needed was to be seen talking to Kent McCord— or his doppleganger. She'd already lost half her business, a few friends, including one she'd been very close to, and her good name in this town. She was sure those who'd seen them chatting away on Main Street would assume the worst.

And Hannah Calhoun still wasn't used to anyone thinking the worst of her. A good girl pleaser all her life and then wham—canceled.

Danny was dressed for the weather in his fleece suit, so he'd be fine for the fifteen minutes she'd grant this man. She needed to catch her breath, get control of herself and decide if "Chase Dawson" was telling the truth. No one had been a better liar, Academy Award level, than Kent, so she couldn't be sure, even with that slight difference of the shape of their eyes and the lack of that scar. *Could* two people who were not identical twins look so much alike?

If this was Kent and he was making a fool of her, God help him. Not that she could do much more than throw a dirty diaper at him. But still.

The coffee truck was right where it always was, a comfort in this sudden craziness.

She stopped at the side of the truck and turned to the man beside her. "If Pete, who owns the truck, sees you, not only won't he serve you, but he may come after you with a shotgun for how you—*Kent*," she said, emphasizing the name, "treated me and a whole lot of other people in this town. Why don't you head over to that bench just down the path, and I'll join you in minute with our orders."

He sighed. "Coffee with cream and sugar. And thank you."

Huh. Kent drank his coffee black and would never let added sugar enter his body. She watched the Kent look-alike head down the path until he disappeared around the curve, then she pushed the stroller to the truck and got their orders, his regular and her iced coffee with a mocha swirl. Pete came out with the drinks in a carboard holder, oohed and aahed over the sleeping Danny, and she balanced the tray on the hood of the stroller.

As she approached the bench where Chase/ Kent was sitting, he stood to take the tray from the stroller, waited for her to sit, then sat beside her—at a distance she appreciated. He sipped his coffee, and she sneaked in another study of his face. She could more readily see the slight differences between him and Kent. There was just something more intense about Chase Dawson's features.

"What exactly did Kent McCord do to make everyone hate his guts?" he asked.

She took a sip of her own drink and set it between them on the bench. "He was a classic con man and swindled a lot of people out of either money or their self-respect. But he was always smart about it. Made it seem like their fault instead of his. Most people he conned just handed over money, no clue he was lying to him."

"And I have the misfortune of looking exactly like this guy."

Well, in this town. But it was hardly misfortune to be that damned good-looking, tall and sexy. Hannah, who'd never slept with a man on the first date, let alone even the usual third, had been suckered into stepping out of her cautious ways for a change.

Don't think about it, she told herself. *How he hurt you. How easily fooled you were when you thought you were a smart cookie and a good judge of character.* She'd dated him for *two* months without a clue. She shook her head at how impossible that seemed now. It was why so many people in town had a hard time believing she hadn't known that he was a con man.

But she'd gotten conned too.

She took another sip of her iced coffee. "He had a secret gambling addiction that got him desperate, apparently. Kent had done so much damage by the end that the police finally started an investigation. He fled town almost a year ago—when I was three months pregnant. No one's heard from him or seen him since. Until today."

He paused with his coffee headed toward his mouth. He looked truly surprised, shocked even. "Do you believe I'm not him?"

She didn't know what to believe anymore. But

the more she looked at him, the more she could the variations in their features. Kent had some trademark moves, too. Like the way he'd toss his hair. How he always sat with his left leg crossed over his right knee. He'd been a tapper, too, drumming his fingers to some imaginary beat on his leg or a tabletop since he used to play the drums in a local band. Small things, but Chase Dawson, if that was really his name, hadn't tossed his thick dark hair once. And he sat with his legs straight down—and not in cowboy man spread, either. Not a single finger tap on the bench or his thigh. "I can see you're not him."

He extended his free hand. "Chase Dawson."

She extended hers, still uneasy. How did this guy look so much like her ex? Her baby's father? "Hannah Calhoun. And this is Danny Calhoun." She ran her gaze over her son, sleeping so peacefully, then took a sip of her coffee. "Anyway, maybe Kent is a half brother you didn't know about? Maybe your mother had a relationship with Kent's father? There has to be some kind of family connection. I mean, you look just like Danny too."

Chase Dawson looked in the stroller, a sense of wonder coming over his face. She well remembered the look on Kent McCord's face when she told him she was pregnant, and it was something akin to horror.

"That's possible," he said. Confusion flashed in his eyes. "Thing is, I look a lot like my mom. Dark hair. Blue eyes. Fair complexion. Why would Kent and I look so much like my *mother*? I guess both his parents have the same coloring."

Now *she* was confused. "Actually, no. Not at all. His mother died years ago when he was very young, but I saw a family photo once, and she was blond and brown-eyed. And his father, Owen Mc-Cord, is tall like the both of you, yes. But he has light brown hair. And hazel eyes. He does have a cleft in his chin, though."

"How could Kent and I look exactly alike and only favor my mother? My mom had had *one* child—me."

Hannah had no idea. "Nothing about this makes sense. But there's a reason a piece of paper with the words *Winston, WY* were among your mother's things."

"Do you know Owen McCord? I mean, is he involved in his grandson's life?"

She nodded. "I wanted my baby to have some connection to his paternal side. I was about six months along when I got up the nerve—even though I'd met Owen a few times at the ranch and even had dinner with him and Kent once. I found Owen in the barn and told him that he was going to be a grandfather."

"How'd he react?" Chase asked, sipping his coffee.

"He broke down crying and hugged me. Then he told me everything Kent had done. His own son had all but destroyed the once prosperous McCord Ranch before Owen had realized it. Secretly sold land, equipment, livestock, made shoddy deals and promises he had no intention of keeping."

"He swindled his own father?" Chase asked with a slow shake of his head.

"Broke his heart."

Chase stood up. "I have to talk to him. There's a very obvious reason why Kent and I look so much alike, why my mother has always been so secretive about my father's identity, why she'd written *Winston, WY*, on that piece of paper, and Owen McCord is the only one who knows what that is. Can you direct me to the ranch?"

Hannah stood too and nodded. She took a final sip of her coffee and tossed it in the trash can near the bench, Chase doing the same.

"I'll do better than that," she said. "I help out on the ranch in my spare time, not that I have much, cleaning out the pens and stalls, spreading hay in the barn, sweeping up. I'd planned to go over now anyway. You can follow me in your truck."

He sucked in a breath. "I appreciate it."

A thought occurred to her, and she whipped around to face Chase. "How old are you?"

"Twenty-eight," he said. "Same as Kent?"

She bit her lip and nodded. "I'd ask you when your birthday is, but I don't know Kent's."

"Did Owen ever mention having another child out there somewhere?" he asked.

"Nope. Kent was an only child just like you."

Chase seemed to take that in. "And his mother died when he was young?"

She nodded. "I don't know anything about her. Kent didn't like to talk about his family much, but that one time he invited me over to the ranch for dinner with him and his father, I saw a family photo on the fireplace mantel of Owen, Kent and his mom, all smiling in front of a duck pond. Kent noticed me looking at it, and I'll never forget the look on his face as he picked it up and stared at it. A wistfulness came over his expression and he'd said, 'I barely remember her.' My heart just went right out to him." She frowned and bit her lip. Maybe that was an act too. Saying and doing anything to get what he wanted."

"I'm sorry, Hannah," Chase said.

"Yeah, me too. But I did get this absolute gift out of the whole mess." She leaned down in front of the stroller and ran a gentle caress over Danny's fleece-capped head.

Chase nodded, his gaze on the baby for a long moment before turning to her. "What's Owen like?"

"A very good person, completely broken still but trying. Between Kent betting against parts of the ranch and fudging the books, Owen ended up in big trouble with the bank, his own employees and other ranchers, who used to be his good friends. The McCord Ranch probably won't ever come back from all Kent pulled."

As they started to walk toward the park exit, Chase pulled his hat down low again.

"You don't know anything about your father?" she asked. "Nothing?"

"I just know my mother was seventeen when I was born. Her parents were not the kindest people, and they tossed her out when the pregnancy she tried to hide became obvious."

Hannah put a hand on his arm. "Your poor mother. How awful." Hannah's parents were gold—the kindest, warmest people—even though they too had gotten their share of dirty looks and "you had to know" from some folks in town, despite having been swindled too. Her family had thick skin and had rallied around Hannah. They'd gotten her through the worst of Kent's betrayal. It hadn't been an easy bunch of months, but when she'd delivered in the hospital, her family and

Owen McCord had been so overjoyed that all the strife had stung a bit less.

They headed out of the park, Chase pulling his Stetson even farther down over his face. "My mother told me she got by lying about her age and waitressing and then went, all alone, to a sliding-scale clinic when it was time to give birth," he said. "When I was little, I'd ask her about my dad and she'd clam up and say I'd have to make do with just a mom who loved me more than anything else in the world. She'd get all teary and I'd feel bad and stop asking questions. She was a great mom. Struggled, but always put me first."

"Oh, Chase. I hope you get answers from Owen."

"Me too," he said.

He kept his head down as they approached his truck.

"The ranch is about five miles out from here. My car's over there," she added, pointing at the old but trustworthy little Honda a few spots up.

"I'll help you load the stroller," he said, walking over with her.

She appreciated the thoughtfulness. "Thanks." She unlatched the five-point harness and lifted Danny out, then settled him in his car seat in the back.

Chase folded up the stroller and put in the trunk.

"I'll be right behind you," he said with a slight tip of his hat. Then he went back over to this truck.

As she buckled her seat belt, she wondered if she should call Owen and prepare him for the Kent look-alike about to barrel into his life. *Was* Owen McCord Chase Dawson's father? If he was, it was entirely possible that he had no idea he had another son.

One who looked just like Kent? And the same age?

Nothing about this situation made any sense.

Just what would Chase Dawson find out at the ranch?

Chapter Two

As Chase followed Hannah's car through the open wrought-iron gates to the McCord Ranch, he could see how vast the property was, ridges in the distance that were probably once full of grazing cattle now empty. About twenty head of cattle were in a large fenced pasture, a smaller pasture with six sheep beside it. Up ahead he could see one lone cowboy, too young to be Owen McCord by a good twenty-five years, unloading hay from a pickup into a huge red barn, which had seen better days.

Was his father somewhere on this property? An actual living, breathing, walking, talking person instead of the abstract concept he'd been for Chase's entire life. For twenty-eight years, the word *father* had no meaning, no name attached, no face, no connection or history. Now, any second, he could very well meet the man he'd wondered about every single day. A lump grew in Chase's throat, butterflies fluttering around his stomach. When he met Owen—and if he *was* Chase's father—would he feel something? Or would Owen McCord seem like a stranger?

The main house caught his attention as he followed Hannah's car toward it. Majestic and situated on a bit of a rise, the white two-story farmhouse had a stately look, but there was no upkeep around it.

His father's house.

Not that anything was for sure yet.

Still, Chase got a chill. He glanced through the windows but didn't see anyone inside, certainly not a man in his late forties who just might be his father. A bit farther up the road, Hannah pulled into a parking area across from the barns, one pickup truck there. Farther along the road he could see a grouping of cabins, probably for ranch hands and empty if the lack of people working the ranch was any indication.

He parked beside Hannah and pulled his hat even farther down, not that there was anyone around to throw beer bottles at him. Hannah emerged from her car and had the stroller out of the trunk before he could move a muscle. She took Danny out of his car seat, giving him a snuggle, and then settled him in the stroller. The baby was awake now, his blue eyes open and alert. She wheeled him over to the driver's-side window of his truck. Now that Chase could see the little guy more clearly, the resemblance between the baby and himself was startling. Danny could easily be Chase Dawson's son.

Not in reality, of course. His last relationship, which hadn't ended well, had been over a year ago. He was no one's father. No one's son. No one's significant other.

"Do you want to just sit for a while to get your bearings or just go talk to Owen?" she asked.

He turned off the ignition. "I've been after the truth of my life since I was a kid. But now that I just might get answers, I can't seem to get out of the truck.

She nodded. "I get it."

Sit here for a while, maybe an hour or two, questions churning in his gut, or just go talk to the man who held the answers?

Now Chase lifted his face to the sun for a moment, letting the warmth combat the shivers running up and down his spine. "Will I find him in the main house?"

She shook her head. "The big barn most likely at this hour. I'm going to show Danny the lambs in the small barn and then do some work in there. So that's where you'll find me...after."

He nodded and got out of the truck, pulling the hat far down again. He glanced over at the smaller outbuilding, then back at Hannah. "Well, here goes." With a last look at Danny, he headed for the big red barn, finding himself walking slower than usual. He stopped and turned. "Hannah?"

She was halfway toward the small barn with the stroller and turned around.

"Thank you. I'm not sure I've said that."

She gave him something of a smile—for the first time since he'd met her—and nodded, then continued on.

He walked across the gravel road to the barn, the young guy who'd been unloading hay gone now. The two big doors were open enough for him to walk right in. The barn was huge, like at the Dawson Family Guest Ranch where he worked, but had a fraction of the usual equipment lining the walls and shelves, and the stalls were empty, which meant the small herd in the pasture was likely all that was left.

He continued down the walkway, sunlight

coming through the huge windows on either end. He stopped when he saw a man, his broad back slightly bent, mucking out one of the stalls. Chase could only see his profile, but he looked to be in his midforties. He had thick light brown hair, like Hannah had said Owen had, and wore jeans, a flannel shirt, a dark green down vest and work boots.

Chase sucked in a breath and took off his hat. "Owen McCord?" he called out.

The man turned and looked at him, gasped, then froze. He dropped the rake and came out in the walkway, his expression barely containing rage. But as he walked up to Chase, confusion crept into his narrowed eyes. Owen stared hard at him and slowed his pace, studying him the way Hannah had.

"Kent?" Owen asked, uncertainty tinging his deep voice. He came a step closer, his head tilting. Chase could clearly see the man immediately knew there was something different about the Kent look-alike who stood before him.

The way a father would.

Took him a minute to find his voice, that lump back in his throat. "My name is Chase Dawson. I'm from Bear Ridge." He left it at that.

Owen's face went pale, one hand flying to this mouth, the other to his chest.

"My mother, Lynne Dawson, died a couple months ago," Chase said. "My entire life I've never known the identity of my father, his name, anything about him. She wouldn't tell me a thing. But I found a piece of paper among her important possessions with just the words *Winston, WY*, on it. And the scrap paper looked old, like she'd had it for years. Thought I'd follow up on the potential lead."

Some color came back into Owen's face. "To your father."

Chase nodded. "Is that you? Is that why I apparently look so much like someone named Kent McCord that I almost got the stuffing kicked out of me the minute I arrived in town?" He explained about the incidents—and meeting Hannah.

"Oh gosh, Hannah," Owen said, his eyes closing briefly. "She must have nearly fainted at the sight of you."

"Are you my father?" Chase asked again.

Owen stared at him for a second, then nodded, so many emotions in his hazel eyes, in his face. "Let's go talk in the house."

Just like that, one brief nod, and Chase knew who his father was. Was right in front of him, not two feet away. For a moment he just stood there, stunned, much like Owen seemed to be.

"I have a terrible story to tell you," Owen said, finally moving toward the doors.

Chase glanced at him. There were tears brewing in Owen's eyes. "Well, I figured it couldn't be good."

They stepped out into the sunshine, and Chase put his hat back on. Owen was quiet as he led the way to the ranch house, barely a quarter mile from the barn. Chase followed him up the porch steps to the front door and then inside. The interior was a lot like the barn's: sparse. The large living room had two wing chairs, no rug, and there were square and rectangular grayish lines on the walls where paintings must have hung. Thinking back to what Hannah had said, Chase wondered if Kent had sold the furnishings out from under his father or if Owen had sold things out of necessity. The bones of the house were beautiful, but the stark emptiness spoke volumes and matched the expression of the man who was walking into the large country kitchen.

"Why don't you have a seat?" Owen said, gesturing at the round wood table by the window. "I'll make coffee."

Chase sat down, watching Owen as he went over to the coffee maker. So far, nothing about the man felt familiar. He didn't see traces of himself in Owen's face. Their coloring was different. Only the height was the same. Maybe the jawline too.

This man is my father, he thought, expecting some sort of rush of emotion. The word itself seemed monumental, but Chase didn't feel anything. Maybe that would come.

Maybe after the "terrible story," Chase would feel *too* much.

Owen set down two mugs, sliding one over to Chase, then brought over a container of half-and-half, a box of sugar packets and two spoons. As Chase fixed his coffee, Owen said, "In case you never want to talk to me again after hearing the story, I want you know I'm sorry. I've been sorry every day since."

That chill raced up his spine again. Chase paused in stirring his coffee and stared at Owen, slowly nodding. What was he about to hear about himself? About his mother?

About his father.

Owen wrapped his hands around his mug and looked out the bay window, just empty pasture on this side of the house. "The reason why people mistook you for Kent is because he's your identical twin. You were separated at birth."

Chase almost spit out his coffee.

What? How?

The air rushed from his lungs, and Chase had

to put down his mug since it suddenly weighed twenty pounds. The words echoed in his head. *Identical twin. Separated at birth…*

Owen's hands shook and he put down his mug too. "Your mother and I were seventeen when you were born. Lynne's parents kicked her out of the house when they found she was pregnant—she was about five months along at that point, I was so scared for her, so I finally told my parents about her and the pregnancy."

Chase braced himself. The *why* he and and his twin had been separated was in here somewhere.

Owen sipped his coffee and looked down. "They'd never liked Lynne. My parents were wealthy and owned a very prosperous ranch in Bear Ridge. They thought she was beneath me, not good enough, from the wrong side of the tracks. They paid for her to go a home for pregnant teenaged girls a couple hours away. What I didn't know until the day she gave birth was my parents' plan. My mother told Lynne she could keep one baby and I'd keep one baby."

Chase gasped. *What?*

Owen squeezed his eyes shut for a moment, then opened them, staring down at this coffee. "And then we'd both go our separate ways, and that would be that. If Lynne didn't agree, they'd fight for custody of both twins and she'd have nothing. I'll never forget my mother coldly looking at Lynne and adding, 'Just like you have now, but worse.'"

Chase felt his mouth drop open. First, his mother's own parents had abandoned her. Then the paternal grandparents threatened her and stole one of her twins—one of her *identical* twins.

"I was under my parents' thumb back then, scared of my father's temper and power," Owen continued. "I didn't fight for Lynne or my other son—the twin who I had to leave behind. I just went along with it. I've never gotten over my shame of that. Never." His gaze dropped to the table and he looked about ten years older, his face creasing as he shook his head.

Chase had a long list of questions. Had Owen been in touch with Lynne while she'd been at the home for teenaged mothers? Had he known she was having twins? Had he even loved Lynne? Had he missed her? Had he ever thought about the baby he'd walked away from?

Him. Had Owen, his father, thought about him?

But once again, he couldn't find his voice, couldn't form a sentence. There were too many questions and they just knocked around in his head in a loop, new ones springing in on him constantly.

"So my parents and I took one baby home and

left one with Lynne," Owen continued. "I'm not sure how they even picked which to take," he added, his voice cracking.

Did you ever ask your parents that? he wanted to know, but now wasn't the time for all this. Owen seemed barely hanging on to his composure, a breakdown imminent. And Chase was still stuck on *identical twin*.

I have a brother.

All this time, all these years, I had a brother.

"Within days, my parents sold their ranch in Bear Ridge and bought a similar one here in Winston, five hours away," Owen said. "They hired a nanny for Kent, but when he was two, I ended up getting married to a cowgirl who worked on the ranch and we were a family. It became easier to put…the past out of my head. I think that's why my parents were all for the marriage."

Ah. "So the woman Hannah mentioned as Kent's mother—that was his stepmother. And I assume Kent wasn't told she *wasn't* his birth mother?"

Owen let out a breath and nodded. "Well, she was there from his earliest memories and always called her mama, so we just let him believe she was. She was a great gal. Loved Kent like he was her own, but unfortunately she got very ill and we lost her when Kent was seven."

"Sorry," Chase said.

"In her last days, when I was so heartsick, I told my parents it was their fault, that she was being taken from us because of what we did to Lynne. Because we separated identical twins."

Chase sucked in a breath.

"My mother said at least we each had one baby out of it." He shook his head again, his sorrow evident on his face. "I turned pretty inward then and devoted myself to being a father, learning the ranching business so I could make something of myself and be able to take Kent and get away from my parents. Within a couple years I bought this place and was able to buy more of the land and grow the operation."

"Did you cut off contact with your folks?" Chase asked.

Owen shook his head. "They were doting grandparents, so I couldn't do that to Kent. He'd lost both his mothers," he added on a whisper. "We had Sunday dinner every week, and my parents took him a few days a week."

"Are they still alive?" Chase asked, the lump back. These were *his* grandparents he was asking about. A part of his own very complicated history.

Owen shook his head. "Car accident when Kent was sixteen."

"Sorry," Chase said again. He didn't want to

think more on the subject of his paternal grand-parents. Not right now anyway.

Owen took a long drink of his coffee and looked out the window, seeming both lost in thought and trying not to think at all.

"Is this the first time you've said any of this aloud?" Chase asked.

Owen glanced at him and nodded. "I didn't even tell my wife back then. I didn't want her to change her opinion of me. And how could she not hate someone who did what I did?" His eyes filled then and he dropped his head.

Chase slid a hand over to Owen's, covering it. Owen's head shot up and the tears ran down his cheeks. Chase squeezed his hand, then let it go.

Damn, this was…a lot. A lot to take in. And Owen had lived it.

"I'd go over it in my head every night in bed when Kent was growing up," Owen said suddenly. "If I should tell him the truth. If I should tell him we're going on a road trip and drive down to Bear Ridge to find Lynne. Finally reunite the brothers."

Why didn't you? Chase wanted to know. *How could you not?*

"When Kent was ten, I told my mother I was thinking about doing that, and she said she'd hired a PI a few months back to see what became of Lynne and the baby and that she'd gotten married. She convinced me to leave Lynne be, that maybe I'd end up hurting her marriage. She said I should let her have her family and I'd have mine."

Chase bristled at the obvious lie Owen had been told. "My mother never got married. She was always on her own."

Owen winced. "I'm not surprised my mother lied. A few months after that conversation, I did go to Bear Ridge. I didn't try to get in touch with Lynne. I had to just see you with my own eyes. And I did. I went over to the elementary school and waited for recess and looked around until I saw the spitting image of my Kent. There you were. You looked happy, running around, playing tag with a group of kids. That helped, I suppose. And then I went back home. Not a day went by without my thinking of you, Chase."

Well, there was one answer to a burning question.

"I appreciate knowing that," Chase said. "And the whole story."

"I deserve what a con man Kent turned out to be," Owen said, his voice resolute. "That my own son betrayed my trust, destroyed this ranch, ended decade-long relationships I'd built with other ranchers and businesspeople and friends. He even sold oil paintings I'd commissioned of the ranch right off the walls of this house, lying to my face by telling me he was having them reframed. From farm equipment to livestock—slowly gone, more lies. Until there was no denying what was going on. My foreman tried to tell me for weeks, but I wouldn't believe it of my own son." He shook his head, this time clearly warding off tears. "I deserve everything Kent did to me. For what *I* did to *him*. And you. And Lynne."

"You were seventeen years old," Chase said, surprising himself with his ready defense of this man. "With a father who terrified you. A mother who easily lied to you. You don't deserve misery because of a past you had little control over."

Owen's eyes misted over. "Well, you're a better person than your twin, that's for damned sure. But you were raised by a lovely person, so it's no surprise."

Chase was getting overwhelmed, sensory overload, so he picked up his mug and drained it. Then he stood up. "I think I need to…leave and just sit with all this. Thank you for being so honest. I'm glad I finally know the truth."

Owen stood too. "I'll walk you out." At the door, he added, "I hope you'll come back. I'm sure you'll have questions."

Chase nodded. At the door, he thought about extending his hand, but that felt off, so he just looked at Owen McCord and nodded, and then headed down the porch, aware of Owen's eyes boring into his back. He didn't hear the front door shut until he'd walked quite a distance, not even sure if he'd gone back in the direction of the barns. But then he saw his truck, oddly comforted by the familiarity of it in all this.

Maybe he'd just go sit in the cab until he could actually drive. Not that he felt ready to leave. He did have questions, and he'd have many more once he slept on everything he'd heard today.

He got inside his truck and felt his shoulders sag. He started the ignition so he could lower the windows and suck in the air, then he leaned his head back, his mother's face coming to mind. The terrible deal she'd been given at seventeen. He and his brother both denied a parent and an identical twin. The tragedies of Owen's life.

Awful.

He closed his eyes and let out a deep breath, but a tap on the passenger-side window jolted him.

It was Hannah.

"You okay?" she asked.

He shook his head.

"I live in town," she said. "Why don't you come over," she added, tucking a swatch of her long blond hair behind her ear. "You look like you need a place to decompress, a comfortable sofa to sink into. And a drink. Follow me. I'm not far from the diner."

He couldn't find his voice. He nodded and waited for her to get Danny resettled in her car. She glanced over at Chase with compassion, something else he could use right now.

How he appreciated her in this moment. He followed her down the long gravel road past the main house, out through the gates of the McCord Ranch. He barely registered the miles passing as she turned back onto Main Street, driving to the end of the road where there were just a few shops and businesses, bordered by the woods.

She parked in front of a yoga studio, and he noticed a narrow door between it and the CPA office on the other side, with an intercom and two buzzers.

They got out and he followed her to the dark blue door, Danny in her arms. He could see the name Calhoun and 2A on the intercom.

"We live in a small two-bedroom apartment," she said—slightly defensively, he thought—as she turned her key in the lock. "Owen invited us to move into the main house at the ranch and my parents offered to give up their spare room for us, but…"

She trailed off and took a breath.

He'd been about to offer to carry Danny up the

steep flight of stairs, but an underlying steeliness in her voice stopped him.

"But what?" he asked.

"But I want—*need*—to make my own way," she said. "It's important to me. This place might not seem like much, but it's safe and cozy and has the basics. Danny is only three months old, and his bassinet and changing station fit comfortably in my bedroom. I could have made the small bedroom a nursery, but I like to have him close."

"What do you do for work?" he asked.

"I've been a personal chef and caterer for two years," she said as they headed upstairs. "Ever since I got up the courage to start my own business after working in restaurant kitchens. My parents and Owen both lost enough, and I know they wouldn't take a dime from me in rent. I might not have had much in the bank, but Kent didn't steal anything from me. Other than my trust in people. I'm someone's mother. I'll pay my own way for me and my child. It's very important to me."

Kent had conned her parents, he realized.

He mentally shook his head. Hannah didn't look any older than twenty-five, and she'd been through so much already.

He had an urge to move the swatch of silky blond hair that came loose from behind her ear;

her hands were full, but she blew the strands out of her way.

"I understand," he said. "You're very independent."

She turned her head slightly and nodded.

When she opened the door to her apartment, he looked around the open concept space, a kitchen and living room. Down a hall he could see three more doors, the two bedrooms and a bathroom, he figured.

"It's a nice place," he said, glancing at the two tall windows that looked out over Main Street, at the plush tan sofa with its throw pillows and a big kilim rug on the floor. A playpen was across the room with a playmat and a basket of baby toys and stuffed animals beside it. There were lots of framed photographs on surfaces and the walls. Hannah and a middle-aged couple, blond like she was. Lots of photos of Danny.

He could see her shoulders relax. She was used to defending herself, he could plainly see, used to judgment. She wasn't going to get any from him. Her independence was admirable. But he had a feeling she had a lot heaped on her shoulders.

"Have a seat," she said, gesturing at the sofa. She set Danny in the playpen with a few small toys and then went into the kitchen. "Beer? Wine?" she called.

He dropped down on the sofa, his legs shakier than he realized. "A beer would really hit the spot. "Thanks."

He was right across from a blown-up black-and-white photograph of Danny in a frame on the wall. *My nephew*, he thought.

I have a nephew. I have a father.

And given the state of the McCord Ranch—including Owen McCord himself—plus his baby nephew and Hannah Calhoun's impressive pride and fierce determination, Chase knew only one thing for sure.

That he wasn't going anywhere so fast.

Chapter Three

Hannah tried not to gasp—over and over—as Chase filled her in on all Owen had told him.

Granted, she hadn't known Owen McCord long, just since last year, but she had no inkling of any of this in his past. She hadn't even known he was just seventeen when he became a dad; she always thought Owen married and had Kent when he was nineteen, which was still very young.

A reminder that you never knew what someone's story was, what was behind their closed doors or shuttered heart.

"Maybe I shouldn't be telling you Owen's life story—a story he never told anyone, not even his wife," Chase said, taking a long sip of the bottled beer she'd given him. They sat in the living room, both on the sofa, on opposite ends, the beer for him, iced tea for her, a plate of untouched key lime pie in front of both. He leaned his head back on the cushion. "But it's also Danny's family background. He has an uncle, and I think he has a right to know that. Even if he is only three months old."

Hannah nodded and hugged a throw pillow to her. "Kent was in the dark his entire life. About *both* his mothers. His identical twin brother. Not to mention what his grandparents were capable of." She shook her head, trying to make sense of Owen's parents making the decisions they had. "I don't want Danny growing up with family secrets lurking."

He glanced at the framed photos on an end table. "Are those your parents?" he asked.

She glanced at the photo of the Calhouns, her mom holding Danny when he was just a week old, her dad looking at his grandbaby with such love in his eyes. "Yup," she said. She smiled, but then it faded. "My parents are in their late fifties. My dad always used to talk about retiring and how they'd rent an RV and travel the US. But Kent conned them out of more than half their savings." Tears poked her eyes, and she blinked them back. "I'm lucky they still speak to me."

"I'm so sorry, Hannah. He really had people fooled."

She nodded. She knew her parents didn't blame her, but she blamed herself. The income from her home business had been cut in half because several of her steady clients had let her know her services would no longer be required. Half of her earnings went into a special account that she'd give her parents when they hit retirement age. It wouldn't make up for the loss, but it would help. After paying her rent and monthly bills, she barely had anything left. But she had what she needed.

"And is that your sister?" he asked, gesturing at another photo on the mantel. "She's the non-blonde in the family?"

Hannah didn't even have to look to know which one he meant. There was only one photo of her and Jasmine. It was hard to look at, but Hannah couldn't bear to put it away. It gave her hope, as if one day, they'd be friends again.

"Nope," she said, picking up her iced tea. "I'm an only child. That's Jasmine. She was like a sister but we had a falling out."

"Let me guess. Because of Kent."

She nodded. "Jasmine got engaged when I first starting dating Kent, and he talked her and her fiancé into letting him invest the money they planned to use for the wedding. He talked a good game and went on and on about how his investments doubled the business at the McCord Ranch. Of course, now we all know what a lie that was. And when Jasmine and her fiancé went to see him about cashing out, he claimed the market was volatile and if they'd wait, it could spring back. By the time they realized something wasn't right, he was gone."

"Jasmine blamed you?"

"More that she believed I had to know Kent was a con man and let him steal their wedding money. She insisted there was no way I—a previously good judge of character—couldn't have known. But I didn't know. Just like Owen didn't know. Kent was that good at his game."

"And this is my identical twin brother," he said, shaking his head.

She blinked back tears again. She'd been hurt when she'd lost clients, hurt by the dirty looks on Main Street, devastated by how he'd conned her parents, but the ache left from Jasmine's refusal to speak to her felt fresh every day. Her best friend since second grade.

"I was devastated that Kent stole their money," she said, taking a sip of her tea because she felt her voice catching. "I was so embarrassed that I'd ever trusted that man, had felt so close to him when he was nothing but a lie…" She let out a breath and leaned her head back, not wanting to rehash all that. But the lump in her chest, that pang in her heart—ever-present.

"If he conned all these people," Chase said, "then why wouldn't they understand that he'd conned you too?" he asked.

She brightened a bit that the thought had occurred to him. "I tried that approach. But Jasmine, my clients, acquaintances, they were just too angry. Kent had fled and there I was."

"You said Kent left town nine months ago. Has your business picked up? Have people come around?"

She shook her head. "Before his lies became clear, I had so many clients that I couldn't even take new ones. I was so excited about my future. But more than half of them fired me. And the ones I couldn't take on? They were no longer interested. I'm down to five or six regular customers."

Thank God for them. She thought about Estie Parker, her retired fourth grade teacher, who'd had a standing order of blackened swordfish with rice every Friday, her and her husband's favorite dish. When Kent had first left town, Estie had hugged her and told Hannah she knew the mean gossip wasn't true and that Hannah couldn't possibly have known Kent's true nature.

"Some people hire me to cook for them for the

entire week," she added, trying to pep herself up with the clients she still had. Madeline Pearson, divorced accountant whose office was next door, hated to cook and had Hannah make and deliver nutritious, delicious easy-to-reheat dinners for five every Monday morning. "I handle all diet plans, food restrictions, allergies, you name it. I've started advertising more on social media to reach people across the county. Yesterday I drove an hour to deliver four gluten-free pies. But I need the money." She'd long reached the point where she needed to take on a part-time job as a cook so that things weren't so tight. But that meant child-care costs—and she couldn't afford that.

A cry came from the playpen, and Hannah jumped up, glad for the interruption. Chase Dawson had come into her life just hours ago and here she was, telling him all the things that brought tears to her eyes when she least expected it—in the grocery store, while folding Danny's onesies and in bed late at night when she couldn't sleep.

Chase stood too. "Can I pick him up?" he asked. "My first act as uncle."

That got a smile out of her. This Chase Dawson had a kind heart, that she could tell. By his retelling of what Owen had told him, particularly. There had been a surprising lack of bitterness in his voice. And now, he wanted to pick up her fussy baby. "Sure."

He smiled back at her, warm and kind and comforting.

She was aware of him following her across the room. She leaned over the playpen. "Who's all fussy," she murmured to her son, all the talk of the past hour suddenly gone from her head. That was how it was with Danny. He commanded her focus, changed her mood, brought sunshine when her heart, mind and soul were full of gloom. Even when he was screeching.

"I've got a slew of baby and toddler cousins at the ranch where I work as the foreman," he said. "I've done my share of emergency babysitting. I don't think I'd ever picked up a baby until I started working at the Dawson Family Guest Ranch."

He had Danny snuggled in his arms in seconds, the baby now content, his blue eyes fixed on Chase. "He's so light but so sturdy at the same time," Chase said, wonder in his voice. He walked over to the window. "Look how overcast it is outside, Danny. Gray skies. Probably going to rain. You're gonna like running through the puddles in about a year and a half."

Hannah could feel the tension seeping out of her. She'd barely gotten past accepting that Chase Dawson was a separate human being from his twin. And here he was, doting on her baby son. His nephew.

Thunder suddenly crackled in the sky, then another boom.

He glanced at the clock on the wall. It was just past six. "I guess I'd better find myself a hotel or B&B," Chase said, standing and bouncing Danny in his arms. "Any recommendations right in town?"

"There's one B&B and a few guest ranches," she said. "But I have no doubt that Owen would love to have you stay with him. He has four spare bedrooms."

He frowned. "I'm definitely not ready for that. Far from it."

She should have figured that. "You're welcome to stay here," she heard herself say before she could stop herself. On one hand, she found his presence comforting. She liked what he represented to her son. And she knew so much about him. Well, the deep dark secrets. It struck her how she was privy to his entire family history when she didn't know the smallest stuff—his favorite food, color, if he liked thrillers. That could lend a false sense of closeness. She'd have to watch out for that. She *didn't* know Chase Dawson. And she'd learned her lesson in a terrible way about thinking a warm smile and opening up meant anything.

"You sure?" he asked.

No. Not sure. But again, words came pouring out of her mouth. "My second bedroom is very small, but it's set up as a guest room. The bed is comfortable." She glanced out the window. "You're welcome to stay as long as you need."

A few days, she figured.

"I appreciate that," he said, smiling that warm smile. He turned his attention back to Danny, giving his hair a caress. "Hey, I get to hang out with you more," he said to the baby.

Oh boy. She was a little too appreciative of anyone who was very kind to her son. But she couldn't imagine this man walking out in the dark rain, thunder crackling, finding a place to stay and then being alone with all that "new territory" he'd stumbled into.

Still, she was opening her home to a man she didn't know existed this morning. Which meant she *hadn't* learned her lesson.

Chase dashed out to grab his duffel from his truck. He hadn't been sure how long he'd be in Winston, how quickly—or not—he'd find information, if any, about his father. He had a week's worth of clothes. Enough to stick around for at least that long.

When he came back into the apartment, Danny was in a baby swing in the kitchen, watching the mobile spin just above him, and Hannah was at the stove, pouring fresh pasta into a big pot of boiling water.

"Spaghetti carbonara?" she asked. "It's been a crazy day, and I need something rich and comforting. I have Italian bread too."

"Sounds good to me. Can I help? I'm a decent enough cook."

"Oh yeah? You can chop prosciutto then," she said with a smile, reaching into the refrigerator and pulling out the package.

As she whisked together eggs and Parmesan in a bowl at the counter, she glanced over at his work. Not bad at all. He selected the right pan for the job from the overhead rack and started the prosciutto sizzling. "Impressive," she said with a smile. "I'll let you chop the garlic," she added, nodding at the basket.

Chase soon had the garlic in the pan. The smell in the small apartment was heavenly. He eyeballed the garlic and prosciutto and when Hannah asked him to check if the spaghetti was ready, he tried a strand, then used a colander to drain the pasta. He poured it into the pan and gave it a good stir.

Hannah added the egg and Parmesan and some salt and pepper, and a little of the pasta water.

Then they were sitting at the kitchen table, two big plates in front of them, along with a basket of the cut up Italian bread and a little bowl of rosemary olive oil.

He took a bite. "Delicious. If I do say so myself."

She laughed. "It is good."

"Well, I expect that from you, a professional chef," he said. "A few times we were short-staffed in the guest ranch caf, and I helped out in the kitchen. I got pretty good at the basics."

She bit her lip and glanced at him. "I wish Owen were here," she said. "I picture him all alone in that big house, dinner for one, which is probably a frozen entrée. Then early to bed and early to rise, each day the same—trying to save the ranch."

"It's nice how much you care about him," Chase said. "I honestly don't know what I think about what happened—the reason we all got separated—but Owen was very forthcoming, even with the details. I appreciate that."

"You finally have answers to questions you've had your entire life."

He nodded. "And now what do I do with the information?" He paused with his pasta-laden fork midway to his mouth. He hadn't meant to say that aloud.

"Don't you want to get know Owen?" she asked. "He's a good man. Definitely honest. You can always see how he feels right on his face."

Yeah, he got that sense too. And maybe it was wrong of Chase to wish Owen had fought for his mother, had fought for *him*.

If not right away, then later.

If Chase were honest, that Owen hadn't, that he'd just continued on with his life as if he didn't have another child out there, bothered him. Not when Owen was seventeen or newly married and still under his parents' thumb. But later.

He took the bite and leaned back in his chair. "Part of me does want to get to know him. But I feel no connection to him—at all."

He noticed her tense up before she looked at him.

"I hate that *that's* the way Danny will think about his father," she said, her eyes troubled. "I'm assuming Kent *won't* be back. That he's long overseas, living very well, swindling more people, always having to flee farther and farther from the last con."

Chase shook his head. He could still barely process that the man she was talking about was his own brother.

Three-month-old Danny Calhoun might not have his father in his life—and Chase hated the cold hard fact that there would be a terrible story for his nephew to hear one day—but he had a devoted mother, a grandfather...and an uncle.

He looked at Danny in the baby swing, the blue eyes just like his, the dark hair. Chase felt no connection to his identical twin, either, likely because he was a terrible person. And the lack of connection to Owen was probably because an estrangement from birth wasn't easy to overcome. He and Owen McCord were strangers.

But Chase felt a bond he couldn't explain with Danny.

"If you make me a list of things Danny could use," he said, "I'll take care of it." He caressed the baby's soft hair.

She tilted her head and then took a long drink of her iced tea. "He has what he needs."

"I know," he said. "I'm talking about extras. And I'm offering because I just discovered, today, that instead of having no paternal family, I not only have a father, I have a baby nephew. That means something to me, Hannah."

She seemed to be taking that in. "Well then," she said, her expression softening. "He likes being held and hoisted in the air."

He glanced at her. "I was talking more along

the lines of a state-of-the-art baby swing or a stroller with all the bells and whistles."

"I'm not one for bells and whistles."

"Hoisting you up in the air, it is," he said, standing and unbuckling Danny from the swing.

The baby giggled, an adorable sound.

"What? You want more of that?" Chase asked Danny. He lifted him and up down four more times, Danny laughing that impossibly loud laugh for a three month old. He was about to lift him again, but the thoughts banging around in his head since he'd talked to Owen came rushing back.

He put Danny back in the swing and sat down. "I can't stop thinking of something."

"What?" she asked, taking her last forkful of pasta.

"Owen said he'd mentioned to his mother that he wanted to go see my mom and me when I was a kid," Chase said. "And that she told him she'd hired a PI to look into what became of us and that my mother had gotten married and he should let well enough alone—a total lie"

He shook his head, unable to process the depths of his own grandparents' deception. And the cruelty. He'd thought his maternal grandparents were uncaring and awful? When his mother had sought to come back home with her newborn, bereft, devastated and alone in the world, they'd informed her they'd sold their home and had moved to California. Chase had never even met them. But they had nothing on the McCords.

He pushed his pasta around his plate, his appetite gone. "I can't help but wonder what might have happened if Owen's mother hadn't interfered."

Hannah reached over and covered his hand with hers for a moment. Her soft, warm touch sent goose bumps up his arm to the nape of his neck. "All I know is that you two are here—finally reunited. You and Owen have a second chance," she added, her hazel-green eyes focused on him. "Nothing can make up for the first twenty-eight years. But you've got now and the future."

He nodded, but the words seemed to bounce off him instead of penetrate. Maybe because his tie to Owen McCord felt like DNA and nothing more. And maybe because of the brick wall long erected in his chest.

He'd take it one day at a time. Including being right here…with this fiercely independent, intriguing woman who felt like something of a lifeline.

Chapter Four

In the morning, just after 6:00 a.m., someone was pressing the buzzer on the intercom for Hannah's apartment—at least five times so far. Whoever it was obviously didn't know she had an infant who never slept past five thirty and that they didn't have to lean on the buzzer to wake her up.

She was in her bedroom, just finishing feeding Danny in the rocker by the window. She set the bottle on the little round table and stood up. Who could possibly be here this early? With such urgency? Particularly someone who didn't know she'd be awake at this hour?

Because of her guest, she'd quickly changed

from her pj's, which were just an old T-shirt and
loose yoga pants, into a sweater and jeans, the
moment she heard Danny's first cry a half hour
ago. Now, she was extra glad she had. She got
up, shifting the baby in her arms and pulled open
her bedroom door—just as Chase had his hand
poised to knock.

"Someone sure wants to see you," he said, gesturing his thumb toward the intercom.

It buzzed again. Then again.

"I can't imagine who." She hurried to the intercom and pressed the Talk button. "Hello?" she
said.

"It's Mom," came the voice of Bettina Calhoun.
A very *strained* voice.

Uh-oh, she thought as a figurative lightbulb
turned on over her head. She should have known
her mother would have heard the gossip: that
"Kent McCord" was not only—supposedly—
back, but had been spotted chatting with Hannah,
who'd had Danny in his stroller, right in front of
the coffee shop. Someone else could have reported
they'd seen Kent and Hannah go into the park too.

And then into Hannah's apartment building—
last night. And that he hadn't emerged.

Her mom wouldn't have called or texted—she
would have charged right over once she heard.

Hannah was surprised the gossip had taken this long to reach her mom.

"Um, coming down," Hannah said.

"Oh, I'll come up," Bettina insisted.

Hannah did not buzz her mother in. "I'll be right down, Mom," she rushed to say, and slipped her feet into her sneakers.

"I'll watch Danny," Chase said.

"That's okay," she told him. "My mother will freak out if I come down without him because she knows I'd never leave him alone in the apartment—and that someone must be watching him. Namely you. And by you, I mean Kent."

"Understood," he said. "Well, I'll hold him while you put on your jacket."

She handed Danny over, then grabbed the red leather jacket and slipped it on. "Oh," she said. "Danny will need his fleece."

Chase looked around and spotted it lying atop the basket of his toys. He snatched it up, then helped get Danny into it.

"Thanks," she said. "I always need four hands."

Which made her aware how helpful it was having Chase Dawson around.

Chase gave Danny back to her and opened the door for her. She gave him a tight smile, then headed down the flight of stairs.

"Good luck," he called.

Okay, this was very strange. Helpful, but strange.

She sucked in a breath, then heard the door close.

Also strange. She was leaving a near stranger in her apartment.

As she got close to the bottom of the staircase, she could see her mother with her nose practically against the glass panel of the front door, her hands cupped around her eyes to peer in. When Bettina saw Hannah, she straightened up, her expression anxious.

Hannah pulled open the door and stepped out in the bright sunshine, a balm after last night's hours-long rain. She'd barely gotten any sleep— because of her guest and the unexpected revelations of yesterday. The rain had been a comfort as she'd sat in the rocker by the window, twice in the middle of the night for Danny's feedings, then just holding him long after he was asleep, that sturdy little weight Chase had noted so soothing against her.

"He's back?" her mother said, half shaking her head, half holding it. "Oh Hannah. Tell me everything. Leave *nothing* out. Here," she added, reaching for Danny. "I'll hold him so you can talk without distraction." Before she could even fully transfer the baby to her mom, she launched into a round of questions. "Why didn't you call me right after? I had to hear this from Suzannah Fielding during my power walk this morning in the park."

Hannah sighed inwardly. Suzannah Fielding was among the group conned by Kent.

"Honestly, I'm surprised she didn't track me down at work yesterday to tattle on you," Bettina added.

Her mother worked full-time as a bank teller at Winston Savings, a job she'd gone back to after eighteen years as a stay at home mother and then the last seven as a volunteer at the animal shelter and hospital, reading stories to admitted children.

Because of Kent.

Because of her daughter.

That her mother was flipping out was understandable.

"It was after three thirty," Hannah said. "But it's also not what you think. That wasn't Kent I was seen talking to."

Her mother looked confused. "Suzannah said she saw him with her own eyes—right in front of the diner. And that Tish Gomez's aunt told her she saw you walking into the park."

Hannah sighed again. "Have I got a story for you. But we'd better go sit down, Mom. It's a doozy."

Her mother's eyes widened. "Have you eaten?

Let's go to the diner and talk. It's so early no one will be there, and I still have that twenty-five-dollar gift card the hospital staff gave me on my last day."

Hannah tried to keep the frown off her face. Bettina had loved volunteering to read stories to kids facing tests and procedures, distracting them, cheering them up, being a bright spot in their day, giving their parents and caregivers a break. And she'd had to leave to work at the bank. To bring in income. Granted, her mother enjoyed the bank, the constant chitchat. Even though Bettina was related to Hannah, aka "she *had* to know!", everyone knew her parents had lost half their savings to Kent. So her association by DNA to Hannah hadn't hurt her parents' standing in town.

Hannah wouldn't have been able to bear it if it had.

They headed down Main Street to the diner, which opened at 6:00 a.m. Hannah realized she should let Chase know this was no quick chat and she'd be a good hour, but she didn't have any way to contact him. Hannah didn't have a landline, just her cell phone, and she didn't have his number. She'd have to rectify that.

Hannah held the door to the diner open for her mom, who'd been thankfully right about few patrons at this early hour. She led her mother toward the back and slid into a booth facing the wall, which suited her. Bettina always liked facing the room.

The waitress came over with an infant seat, and her mom had Danny out of his fleece suit and secured in moments. Fortunately, the waitress was new in town and likely had no idea who Kent McCord was at this point. After all, it had been nine months since he'd left town, and though people still talked about what happened, it wasn't a hot topic.

Until yesterday, of course. And this morning.

Hannah ordered the blueberry pancakes and coffee. Her mother went for the western omelet and rye toast, also coffee.

Once they were alone, Hannah explained what happened yesterday. From the moment she spied who she thought was Kent, to someone throwing a wadded-up fast food wrapper at him from a car, to taking him over to the McCord Ranch and all that had been revealed there. And then how Chase Dawson ended up sleeping in her guest room.

And was still in her apartment.

Her mother's eyes had gotten wider and wider as Hannah talked.

"Oh my God," Bettina said, shaking her head in disbelief.

"I know."

The waitress returned with their coffee. Hannah and her mother both drank it in a few gulps.

"What's he like—Chase?" her mom asked, signaling the waitress to bring over the coffeepot.

Hannah thought about that for a moment. "He's…either wonderful or too good to be true."

"What makes him—" Bettina started to ask but clamped her lips shut while the waitress refilled their mugs. As soon as the woman left, her mom added, "Wonderful?

Hannah wrapped both hands around the warm mug. "Aside from just his *way*—kind, easy to talk to, helpful, considerate—he felt an instant connection to his little nephew. The relation means something to him. Especially, maybe, because he's ambivalent about Owen and how he feels about the story."

"It's some story. Jeez," her mother said, shaking her head again. Her way of processing.

The waitress returned with their meals. Hannah wasn't sure if she'd have an appetite but sharing everything that had happened with her mom had taken a weight off her shoulders. She wanted her mother's opinion of everything. Including Chase Dawson himself. *If* he was too good to be true. If she should be on guard. She said as much to Bettina as she poured maple syrup on her pancakes.

"On guard from…?" her mother asked, one

blond eyebrow raised. "I mean, given that he looks just like Kent, I'm surprised you don't want to shove a pie in his face. Are you saying you're attracted to him?"

Hannah froze for a second. *Was* she? The idea of that seemed...complicated. "Well, Kent was very good-looking, so you know Chase is. But it's not that. When I look at Chase, I don't see Kent. I only see the variations in their features, where Chase's are more intense. I see their *differences*. I don't see Kent at all."

Her mother paused with a bite of omelet almost to her mouth. "So you are attracted. Because if he did remind you of that rat bastard, you probably wouldn't have invited him to stay with you."

Hannah thought about that for a moment too, taking a bite of her pancakes. Was she physically attracted to Chase? Was that even possible, given that she'd just had a baby three months ago? She'd only just recently begun to feel that she was laying claim to her body again, which still had its squishy areas.

Yes, he was very good-looking. And tall and lean and muscular. But what drew her was his kindness. The type that couldn't be faked. It was in his eyes, in his gestures, in his voice.

The way he looked at his nephew—with wonder and even a sense of hope—was the clincher.

She tried explaining that to her mom. "But it's all beside the point anyway since I'm not getting involved with any man. Possibly ever."

"When you're ready, honey," Bettina said with an assured nod, and then spread orange marmalade on her rye toast.

"I can't imagine ever being ready. How could I ever trust a guy again?"

Her mother put her toast down, reached over and squeezed her hand. "Hannah, you don't have to make any pronouncements or absolutes. Kent McCord fooled a lot of smart people—yes, including you. Don't let him steal your faith in humanity too. Or your dreams for your future. You'll be ready when you're ready."

Hannah gave a half-hearted shrug as sadness enveloped her. She didn't want to let her past dictate her future. But right now her dreams were about rebuilding her personal chef and catering business. Raising her son. Paying back her parents.

She didn't know if she'd ever get Jasmine's friendship back. But that was a dream too.

Her mom slid from the booth and sat down beside Hannah, slinging an arm around her shoulders. "You're going to be just fine, Hannah Banana. I promise you. If Chase Dawson can make you smile, then I'm all for him being in your life. A little too close for my comfort, maybe, in that little apartment..."

"You have nothing to worry about—*I* promise *you*. There's absolutely nothing going on between me and Chase. We met *yesterday*, for one. And we both had major zingers thrown at us. We're just a comforting presence to the other because of it. I can answer some of his questions. He can answer some of mine. We both have a tie to Owen. And then there's Danny."

"I've been trying to think of ulterior motives he might have, but based on everything you said, all he has to gain is a possible relationship with the father he never met and a baby nephew."

Hannah nodded. "Exactly."

Her mother patted her arm, then went back to her side of the booth. "Just keep your guard up is all I'm saying. For a lot of reasons."

"I know. And it is. Very much so."

They stopped the heavy conversation so they could actually eat, her mother telling her funny stories about her bank customers, Hannah sharing a not-so-funny story about mixing up oven temperatures a few days ago and burning a gluten-free five-veggie pizza for one of her few clients. She'd scraped off the charred parts and had two slices for dinner—*waste not, want not* was the motto she'd grown up with—then made a new, perfect pizza and delivered it.

Her mom took the last bite of her rye toast, then turned to Danny beside her in the infant seat. "I'm glad you have a nice uncle," she whispered to her grandson.

Hannah smiled. How she loved her mom. She could always count on Bettina Calhoun for support *and* the truth, whether Hannah liked that truth or not. And right now she was pretty sure her mother was saying: *Okay, Buster, so far, so good, but we'll see.*

Hannah couldn't agree more.

The first thing Hannah did when she got back to her apartment was tell Chase they should exchange cell phone numbers, which they did. Then she told him all was well with her mother, that Hannah had explained, and then they'd had a nice breakfast. Right at the scene of the crime and no one had gawked or thrown things at her. Hannah had long avoided going into both the diner and the coffee shop; she had to be frugal anyway.

Necessity sometimes came in handy.

Of course she'd left out the other stuff she and her mom covered. About her possible attraction to him.

As she stood in the living room, talking-distance

from Chase, she thought again that her attraction to him was perfectly understandable. He was a tall, sexy good-looking guy, objectively speaking. But she was done with acting on her attraction to anyone. It hadn't even been a year since Kent had done his damage, both to her personally and a lot of others in myriad ways.

"I'd be happy to hang with my cute nephew if you want some time to yourself or to take a long, hot shower," he said.

This was why she was drawn to him.

"I would love a long, hot shower," she said. "And thanks."

His blue eyes lit up and he took Danny from her, rocking the baby a bit as he walked over to the windows. "Sunny out there," he said. "Good day for a stroll." But his expression faltered and he glanced over at her. "I guess I can't exactly do that in this town—walk around. I'll get yelled at it. Wrappers thrown at me. Elderly ranchers shaking their fists at me."

Hannah frowned. "I didn't even think of that— that we have to alert people that you're not Kent. I wonder what the best way to do that is."

"Where's the hub of town gossip?" he asked.

"The coffee shop, for sure. Right on Main Street. Two blocks from the diner. I suppose we could go there and make an announcement."

He raised an eyebrow and mimicked holding a microphone with his fist up to his mouth. "Hi, everyone, if I may have your attention. I know I look just like the man who conned many of you, your family and friends out of your money and your trust. But I'm actually *Chase Dawson*, his separated-at-birth, long-lost identical twin brother, and I came to town meet the father I never knew. That's real belicvable. Even I can barely believe it."

"It *is* the truth, though," she said. "And it would get the job done."

"Yeah?" he asked. "I was kidding."

"A crazy announcement at prime time at Coffee Catch would reach a lot of people, and then we just need them to spread the word. This is a small town. Everyone who needs to know *will* within a half hour."

"When's prime time?" he asked.

"Every day between seven and ten, noon to two and five to closing at nine. Though I just realized you should clear it with Owen and make sure he's okay with it. He'll be overrun with people asking him if it's true, and then everyone will want to know the story behind the story. How you were separated from Kent and why."

"Owen might not want any of that out there," Chase said. "And I don't blame him. Like he needs more people gossiping about what he had little control over?"

"Yeah, it's hard to say how people will react. I guess some will be compassionate and others will judge him—the ones who've shunned him for the past nine months because they believe he knew what Kent was doing. Even though his ranch was completely decimated. One former rancher friend even accused Owen of faking the huge financial loss to save face, that Kent had Owen's money hidden away in a foreign account."

Chase let out a sigh. Then he hoisted Danny high in the air, earning a baby giggle, then another on the way back down. "Guess I'll be paying your grandpa a visit this morning, Danny."

"It's a lot," she said, her heart going out to him. The situation was complicated. And emotionally charged. For Owen, for Chase—and everyone who'd been affected by Kent.

"Well, turns out I need to go see him anyway," Chase said, giving Danny a bounce. "About another matter, so it's good timing."

Hannah's curiosity was peaked. "Oh?" she asked.

"I had a good hour earlier while you were gone to just think," he said, pointing to the half full coffeepot on the kitchen counter. "I had two strong mugfulls and some toast—hope that's okay."

"Of course," she said. "Help yourself to anything you need."

He picked up the blue mug that bore the Winston Animal Shelter logo and drained it. "I want to get to know Owen. And I also feel compelled to help him. I think I mentioned I'm a foreman at a popular guest ranch up in Bear Ridge. Ranch management, the day-to-day operations, the big and small picture—it's what I do. I want to turn the McCord Ranch around, get it back in the black, even though that'll mean starting small, which is what the McCord Ranch is now, anyway."

Hannah gasped. "Chase, that's great. You'll learn a lot about Owen by just being at the ranch. By soaking up everything in the office and on the property. And of course, by working side by side with him."

"Exactly," Chase said with a nod. "If that second chance—first chance, actually—is going to happen, this would be a solid way there. Working toward something, doing something. Slow and steady, no forced interactions, no walks in the park or awkward dinners."

She smiled. "That sounds really good. The McCord Ranch is Danny's legacy. And yours."

She could tell by his expression that he hadn't thought of it that way. And that maybe he wasn't sure he wanted to go *that* far.

"I didn't think the McCord Ranch would survive even until Danny's first birthday," Hannah said. "But suddenly I feel hopeful."

"Me too," he said, slowly nodding.

This is why I'm drawn to you, dammit, she thought for the third time in the past hour and a half.

Chapter Five

By the time Chase arrived at the McCord Ranch, it was close to 9:00 a.m. Owen had likely been working since at least 5:30 a.m. As he drove up the gravel road toward the parking area, he could see Owen leading six sheep into a far pasture.

He glanced at the cattle grazing in another large field. He counted eighteen.

According to a news article he'd read while doing a simple online search of the McCord Ranch, which focused on Kent being under investigation, the ranch had had over forty employees and almost two hundred head of cattle and fifty sheep. Over two thousand acres had been parsed to eight hundred, secretly sold off to developers by Kent, and already two "model" ranches had been built. From where Chase stood outside the big barn, he could just see the roof of those barns, wrought-iron weather vanes atop. The sight of them must break Owen's heart. All his hard work, over decades, building his own legacy. He probably avoiding looking.

Chase pulled his iced coffee from his truck's console and took a long sip. By the time he returned it, he saw Owen heading over.

As Chase watched him approach, he was struck by how completely unfamiliar this man was. What he expected when he finally met his father, he didn't know exactly. But *something*. A feeling, a burst of something in his chest, in his throat. The word *father* had always loomed large—momentous. But as he looked at Owen McCord, all he saw was a stranger. That would change, Chase knew, as they worked together day by day for the next couple of weeks. But would Owen *feel* like his father?

Maybe Chase was making too big a deal out this. He had no idea what having a father felt like; he only knew what the childhood hole in his heart had wrought as he grew up—wishing, wondering, hoping. Now here it all was. Day by day, he reminded himself.

"I'm glad you came back," Owen called as he neared. He wore jeans, a flannel shirt over a T-shirt, work boots and a dark brown Stetson. "I wasn't sure you would."

"All I know is that you're the father I've been waiting to meet my entire life."

Owen looked at him for a moment and then turned toward the field. Chase had a feeling he was blinking back tears. This *had* to be emotional for him.

"And because of that," Chase said, "I want to help here. I'm the foreman of a guest ranch. Between the two of us, we can get the McCord Ranch back in the black. Not to what it was, of course. But a fresh start. And once the place is thriving again, you can slowly rebuild."

"I'm beyond words," Owen said. "I need help and to have yours means the world to me."

Chase extended his hand, and Owen clasped it with both of his. "This is my nephew's legacy," he said, looking out at the pastures, at the barns. "Let's do this for him."

Owen glanced down at the gravel for a moment, then back up at Chase. "If that's your mindset, and I'm glad it is, you must be doing a world of good for Hannah's spirits."

Hannah. Her pretty face, the sharp hazel-green eyes, her long blond hair, floated into his mind.

"She's very independent," Chase said. "She's made that clear. But my help on this ranch is something she can heartily accept."

Owen nodded. "I can understand that. Her baby boy is everything to her."

And he means a lot to me, Chase thought. Already.

"I suppose you'll want to start with the books," Owen said. "The office is attached to the main house. It has its own entrance around the side, so you can come and go."

Chase nodded. "Sounds good."

He liked the idea of coming and going at will and not having to be in Owen's house where he'd raised only one of his sons. Where, had things been different, Chase might have spent school vacations and summers.

The house gave him the shivers.

They headed to the office, going around the house to the side where there were porch steps leading up to it. A big wood desk, holding just an old-model laptop and a mug with pens and pencils, was in the center, facing toward the door.

"For the last nine months," Owen said as he stood in the doorway, "I've kept perfect records to the penny. You'll find everything labeled in files in the laptop," he said, pointing at it. "There's a coffee maker on the credenza and fixings in the mini fridge."

Chase would need another caffeine boost in a couple hours, no doubt. He went around to the front of the desk and sat down in the big chair, his gaze immediately going to the photos on the surface. One of a much younger Owen, a smiling woman with long light brown hair and a boy who looked just like Chase when he was four or five. There was also photo of Hannah holding Danny.

"If it's hard to look at," Owen said, pointing at the photo of himself, his late wife and Kent, "just throw it in a drawer. I keep it there as a reminder that even though life can throw some major curveballs, there are great times, too. I loved my wife. And Kent at four years old was a sweet and happy little boy."

Chase had so many questions—about Owen's relationship with his parents after they moved to Winston, when, exactly, Kent had started showing he was no longer sweet. But there would be time for questions as the days wore on. Right now, he'd focus on the ranch itself.

"I'll never get over my shame at leaving you behind," Owen said suddenly. "At letting my parents tear us all apart. At not calling your mother and asking if I could see you, if we could reunite you and Kent." He shook his head.

That Owen was torn apart by the past was an understatement. Chase wished he had words to make the man feel better, even if just in this moment, but everything running through his head sounded trite. *Can't change the past...focus on the here and now...*

"I guess my mother must have done a search for you since she had Winston, WY, on that piece of paper," Chase said. "For her own reasons, she must not have felt comfortable going to find you and Kent. Who knows, maybe your mother called and threatened her about ever even considering such a thing."

"Maybe so. Or maybe your mom drove up with sunglasses and a hat pulled down low and went to Kent's school to try to get a look at him. Like I did with you."

Huh. Chase hadn't even considered that for some reason, but of course she must have. Lynne Dawson, so loving, such a good mother, wouldn't have been able to not at least *see* the son she'd lost.

"I used to wonder if Kent would have turned out differently had we all stayed together," Owen said. "If he'd had a twin brother by his side. Or maybe he still would have been a con man. I guess it's dumb to speculate. There's just no way to know. And it's torturous, thinking that way."

Chase looked at Owen, the man's heartache

so raw. He suddenly felt grateful that Owen had Danny in his life, that he had the support of Hannah. Owen seemed so alone regardless, but his grandson and the baby's kind, compassionate mother must bring him joy every day.

Owen stood. "I can't tell you how much I appreciate that you're here, Chase. And that you'll help me get this ranch pointed in the right direction. I just barely get the day's work done and have little left to sell to pull out of the deficits. There's no one to sell to anyway. Folks around here haven't spoken to me in nine months."

A part of Chase wanted to stand up and go hug the man. Chase couldn't change the past, but he could help now and would. For Owen to be blamed and shunned and gossiped about because of his son's actions—which Chase had no doubt Owen knew nothing about—bothered him. A lot.

"I have a plan for that, too—it was Hannah's great idea," Chase said. "I'm going to need to walk around free and clear in Winston without having fists shaken at me. People need to know I'm not Kent. And to do that, I'll need to explain a bit about the estrangement. And provide proof— which I also have a plan for."

Owen stared at him. "Not a soul knows that I had identical twins who were separated at birth. Except now you and Hannah." He sucked in a breath and let it out slowly. "But truth begets truth. So I'm all for your plan."

Chase nodded, his tense shoulders relaxing. "The people of Winston also need to know you were not aware that Kent was not only conning your neighbors and friends, but you as well, that he destroyed the once great McCord Ranch. I'll explain I'm here to help turn the ranch around."

"Where and when are you going to share all this?" Owen asked.

"I want to take care of it early tonight. At the coffee shop around six. Do you want to attend?"

Owen shook his head. "I don't think I could handle the questions just yet. 'Why did you separate identical twins, how could you, I can't believe you walked away from one of your own baby sons'... It'll just make folks hate me more."

Aww, Owen, Chase thought. "If you'll allow it, maybe I can add just enough explanation on that front."

Owen seemed to be thinking about that for a moment. "I trust you, Chase. I shouldn't trust anyone after what Kent put me through, but to be honest, I know Hannah feels like that and I don't want her to be closed off from people like I am. I want her to believe in people, to trust, to get back to where she was *before*. I want to show her I'm willing, you know?"

I do know, he thought, moved by Owen's devotion to Hannah. *But you deserve good things just like she does*. Chase would leave it alone for now. Owen was broken, and helping to piece him back together was going to take some time.

"I'm glad on both counts," Chase said.

Owen gave a nod and quickly left. But a minute later, he was back. "I just want you know you're welcome to stay in the house. Might be too much too soon—I understand if it is." With that, he turned and left again.

Chase was glad Owen hadn't waited for an answer. It *was* too much too soon. Right now, he liked staying at Hannah's. Being able to help her, give her some time to herself. And that's where his tiny nephew lived.

He glanced at the photo of her and Danny on the desk; she was holding the infant close to her face, her expression radiating a happiness he knew only Danny could bring these days, and he immediately felt that surge of protectiveness.

But he was also aware that he found it hard to stop looking at her.

Chase got up and made a pot of coffee, needing that caffeine jolt now—and a distraction as he tried to clear his mind of the people involved here so he could focus on business. He sat back down, and then pored over the ranch files, books, invoices and the four or five business plans Owen had drawn up for loans over the past nine months, each of which had been turned down.

Two hours went by in a snap. Then he left the office and drove around the ranch for another two hours, taking stock of the place *and* photos, stopping to go on long walks along the fenced pastures, visiting the outbuildings to check inventory, of which there was little, and noting the new boundaries of the property. The ranch hand wasn't working today; Chase knew from the files that he only worked two days a week. How Owen had managed with such little help was something. A testament to his fight to save the McCord Ranch. And it fired up Chase even more to get the job done.

He had some solid ideas for how to restructure the operation, and he put it all in an email to Owen so that he could read and digest it, think about it, and form questions or even okay the plans.

Chase got back into his truck and headed out. He had two stops to make before he'd go back to Hannah's place. One involved the police. And the other was a photo shop that he'd researched online. He'd have to drive twenty minutes to Mumford, a larger town, to get what he needed for the announcement at the coffee shop tonight, but it would be worth it.

He knew that the announcement, complete with proof, would take a weight off Hannah's shoulders. Things would change for her and Owen after, even if the change was slow to get going. And he couldn't wait to tell her that he had a good plan for the McCord Ranch and was confident about its future. Her son's future.

That he cared about making Hannah Calhoun happy was just another unexpected revelation since he'd arrived in town.

Hannah had a quiet morning at home with Danny, and once she put him down for his nap, she got busy with her orders, preparing meals for two clients and then making a festive afternoon tea for another client's bridal shower—savory tarts and quiches, dainty finger sandwiches, mini scones and éclairs, and several kinds of tea with all the fixings. She'd just made her last delivery in town and figured she'd take Danny to see the ducks in the park.

As she turned on Main Street, her phone pinged with a text and she pulled into a spot.

Chase.

Productive day the ranch. Also, planning on introducing myself to the town at the coffee shop at 5:30. See you there?

Wouldn't miss it, she texted back.

She was just a few blocks from the park entrance, so she exited her car and got the stroller from the trunk, then took Danny from his car seat and settled him in. She glanced up at the shop she'd parked in front of. Princess for a Day boutique, specializing in weddings and black tie events. In the window was one of the most beautiful wedding gowns she'd ever seen. When she'd first met Kent, she'd daydreamed about their future and had walked past this store often to check out the window displays. She'd always loved every dress. And the veils and shoes. She'd loved wondering about their future, where their relationship would go.

But those fantasies had all been stomped on.

And now Chase Dawson, with his kind ways, was reminding her of dreams she'd had to let go of. Always ready with a helping hand, a kind word, eyes that lit up at the sight of her son when she'd finally stopped wishing her life had turned out differently, that she had a loving husband at her side. She'd faced reality, and reality was Kent.

She couldn't imagine trusting a man again.

She turned her gaze from the shop window, from the beautiful wedding dress she'd never wear, just as someone came out of the boutique, a long gray dress bag over her arm.

Jasmine.

Her former best friend.

Her hair in its trademark long braid down one shoulder, Jasmine wore the green leather moto jacket she'd bought on their road trip to Texas four years ago. Hannah had graduated from a local culinary school and Jasmine's birthday was the same month, so they'd taken off for fun and adventure for two weeks. Hannah had bought her beloved red leather jacket on that trip. She was surprised Jasmine hadn't thrown hers in the trash; surely it must remind her of Hannah, since Hannah's red one always made her think of her best friend, however former, however painful. Maybe Jasmine had a tiny bit of love for her underneath all the anger and accusations that had destroyed their friendship.

A lump immediately formed in Hannah's throat. Would Jasmine speak to her? Even just a hello? Hannah would take a simple pleasantry a stranger would give a passerby if it meant no dirty look and Jasmine crossing the street to avoid her.

"So you're back with that con man, I hear," Jasmine said, her brown eyes full of anger. "Sickening. I knew you knew Kent was a lying dirtbag and didn't care. I knew it!" With that, she came tearing down the steps, struggling to keep from dragging the dress bag.

"That wasn't Kent I was talking to in front of the diner," Hannah rushed to say. "And I *didn't* know Kent was a con man. I don't know how to prove it to you, but I didn't know."

"Why keep lying? If you'd lie about talking to Kent when people saw you two—God, you have no shame." With that, she turned toward the car, parked a few over from Hannah's.

"The man I was talking to, who some *mistook* for Kent," Hannah called to her, "was his identical twin brother. He'll be making an announcement at the Coffee Catch at 5:30 tonight. Please come, Jasmine."

Jasmine stared daggers at her. "Identical twin?" She snorted. "Oh, good one, Hannah. Real believable." She marched to her SUV.

Tears threatened and Hannah lifted her chin. She couldn't let this ruin her day. She'd already told Danny in the car they were going to the park to see the ducks, and they were going.

She wished Chase were beside her right now to put a hand on her shoulder. To just *be* there.

But needing him hardly made her feel better.

Chapter Six

Sunglasses on, Stetson pulled down low, a large shopping bag in each of his hands, Chase opened the door to the Coffee Catch at 5:25 p.m., hoping for a good-sized crowd. He got his wish. The place was packed. A bar with fifteen or so stools was practically filled, and the overstuffed couches and chairs and tables of different sizes dotted around the huge space were all taken.

Perfect.

He saw Chief Trent Durban, who he'd met with an hour ago before he'd gone to the photo shop. The chief, who'd be introducing Chase and confirming a few things during the announcement, waved him over to where he stood at the edge of the counter. The man was commanding—in his midforties, very tall and muscular, with sharp dark eyes, and many medals and ribbons on his tan uniform.

Chase felt a few eyes on him, heard whispers, as he wove his way through the tables and couches to the front of the shop, where the chief stood. He looked around for Hannah but didn't see her, then spotted her coming through the door with her parents, and Danny in his stroller.

The moment he took off his sunglasses and hat, he heard the whispers flying fast and furious and saw a few people pointing at him.

"Chief Durban," someone called out from a table. "You finally caught the bastard." People started turning and looking, and there was a smattering of applause.

"Actually," the chief said, "this man, who arrived in town yesterday afternoon, is *not* Kent McCord." At gasps and murmurs, he held up his hands. "I know, I was surprised as you're all going to be. He's a dead ringer for Kent, and there's a good reason for that. This is Chase Dawson. Kent McCord's identical twin brother."

"Oh, please," a man snapped from the counter. "Kent didn't have any siblings."

"Yeah," another man called. "I've known Owen

McCord for twenty years and he had *one* child—the criminal grifter standing right there."

Chase noticed a woman at a table near the front who picked up half her muffin and seemed about to throw it at him, but then eyed the chief and set it back down.

A bunch of people got out their cell phones and started recording. It would be all over town even sooner than he thought.

"Kent McCord and Chase Dawson are identical twins who were separated at birth," the chief continued. "Identical twins have the same DNA, but they do *not* have the same fingerprints. I have Kent's fingerprints on file from teenage infractions. This afternoon, I took Chase Dawson's fingerprints and called in a favor to the lab to match them—or not. They are *not* a match."

Chase reached into the bags and took out the two blown-up poster board photos—one of himself, one of Kent. He put them on easels he'd bought for the occasion and aimed a pointer at Kent's eyes. "If you look closely, you may be able to see the variations in our features," he said. "My eyes are more intense. Kent's are softer." He aimed the pointer at Kent's eyes. "Kent has a scar by his left eye. I don't."

"Huh," the woman who'd been about to throw

the muffin called out. "I do see the differences now that you point them out."

The chief nodded. "Chase here is Kent's identical twin. I confirmed it with Owen McCord myself, and the fingerprints proved to me that Chase is clearly not Kent."

"How were you separated at birth?" a woman asked.

Chase sucked in a breath. He'd didn't have his own mind wrapped around his birth story; now he was going to share it with all these people?

He glanced around the room. Dead silence, eyes glued to him, waiting to hear just how he'd been separated from his identical twin.

"My mother and Owen McCord were a teenage couple," he said. "They were seventeen when their twin sons were born—and manipulated, cruelly, by Owen's parents. Each parent took a twin home—Owen took Kent. My mother took me. Kent and I didn't know our birth story, and neither of us knew we had a twin."

Murmurs had him pause for a breath.

"How'd you find out?" someone called out.

"I came to Winston because I had a bit of information that my father, whose identity and name I'd never known, might live here. When I arrived, I ran into Hannah Calhoun in front of the diner, and trust me, she thought I was Kent just like you did and gave me a piece of her mind before I finally convinced her I *wasn't* Kent. She led to me Owen, who confirmed he's my father."

He glanced around for Owen, wondering if he'd decided to come after all, but Chase didn't see him. His gaze found Hannah at the back of the room. She seemed anxious, but hopefully that could be put to rest.

"I'd also like to add," Chase continued, "that neither Hannah nor Owen had any idea that Kent was a criminal con man. They were snowed just like many of you. I've known Hannah and Owen for just a short while, but I believe that with all my heart. Many of you have known them for decades."

Eyes swung to Hannah, then the whispers and murmurs began again. Chase saw her mother sling a protective arm around her shoulder.

"I wanted to make this announcement because I'm going to be in town for a while," Chase added, "trying to save the McCord Ranch for my baby nephew—it's his legacy. I know many of you lost a lot to Kent, and there may be no chance of ever recouping that money. And I also know that Owen is heartsick over all this. His own son betrayed him, decimated the ranch he built himself, fled town, and cost Owen his reputation and many decades-long friendships. He didn't want to be here for my announcement, and I understand why. But I want to assure you that everything I said is true."

Chase glanced around, noticing expressions softening.

"You're not bitter about what happened?" a woman asked. "Separated from your own twin and your dad your whole life?"

Chase glanced down for a moment. "My entire life I was torn up over thinking my own father didn't want to know me. I was lucky to have a great mother, who struggled and must have been heartsick till the day she died over getting torn from her other baby. But the past is the past, and I can be bitter or I can start with what I now have. A father I just met yesterday. A baby nephew I already feel a bond with."

There were a lot of nods.

"I appreciate you all listening," Chase said. "It's a rotten story with a rotten ending, but I almost feel like finding that scrap of paper with *Winston, WY*, on it sent me here to change that ending. To turn something terrible into a fresh start for Owen. And for Hannah, who's raising a baby on her own." He met her gaze, but he couldn't tell what she was thinking.

He turned to remove the poster boards and quickly slid them and the fold-up easels into the shopping bag. He turned to Chief Durban. "I can't thank you enough."

The chief shook his hand. "You did great," he said. "I think public opinion will be on your side," he added, then headed to the counter to order something.

Here's hoping, he thought, wanting to go talk to Hannah.

"Sorry my cousin almost punched you out in front of the diner yesterday," a woman said as he passed her table. He recognized her from when he first arrived in town.

Chase nodded. "I understand. I didn't then, but I do now."

He was able to make his way to Hannah without getting peppered with questions because people were either on their phones, reporting the hot gossip, or whispering loudly among themselves about what they'd just learned.

"I think you really helped Owen," Hannah said, her eyes brighter. "Things are going to be much better for him."

"And you," Hannah's mother said to her. She turned to Chase and extended her hand. "Bettina Calhoun. And this is Hannah's dad, Henry." They shook hands too. "We'd love to have you over for dinner soon."

"I'd like that," he said.

A bunch of people came over to shake Chase's hand. After a lot of *Wow, what a story*, there were many apologies to Hannah. *Of course you didn't know. That criminal could fool Einstein.* Chase could see her shoulders relaxing.

Yes, this was a good idea.

He stepped aside to text Owen.

Went well. See you tomorrow.

Within seconds Owen wrote back a simple Thank you.

Three dots kept flashing and disappearing on the screen.

For everything, Owen added.

Chase responded with the smiley face emoji wearing a cowboy hat.

First mission accomplished; it was now time for the next delicate operation.

To help Hannah regain her trust in people.

Hannah and Chase had gotten back to her apartment just twenty minutes ago, Chase wheeling the stroller, which she still wasn't used to, and her mother had already called with a report. Bettina had been stopped, phoned or texted by at least thirty people who were "simply stunned by Chase's announcement" and wanted to apologize for not believing Hannah hadn't known about Kent. Lots of *Of course that dear gal didn't know!*

Nothing Chase had said at the coffee shop could possibly prove that, but everything *else* he'd said, backed by the chief, had tugged on heart-strings and her association with him now made her seem aboveboard.

Life was a little too unpredictable, she thought, checking on Danny with a glance over at him in the baby swing in the corner of the kitchen. People could turn on a dime. Not that she wasn't glad, of course. She'd already gotten two emails from for-mer clients asking if she could fit them into her schedule again. And she had no doubt more would be coming once the gossip machine did its job.

A good thing.

No call or email or text from Jasmine, though, and Hannah wasn't sure she'd hear from her old friend. Jasmine *had* been in the Coffee Catch for the announcement; Hannah had been surprised to see her standing in the back, way on the other side of the space.

You think I'd let my own parents, who you know I love so much, lose half their savings? Hannah had asked when Jasmine kept insisting Hannah had to have known Kent was a con man.

Some people will do anything for love, Jasmine had actually countered.

There'd been no way to defend herself.

She'd seen Jasmine slipping out of the coffee shop as Chase was packing up his poster boards and didn't try to catch Hannah's eye. Maybe Jasmine needed some time to process everything she'd heard, talk it over with her fiancé.

"Dollar fifty for your thoughts," Chase said from beside her in the kitchen.

She startled; she'd been actually lost in those thoughts. "Wow, my mom used to offer me a penny."

"Well, now you know I *really* want to know what has you a million miles away," he said, shooting her that warm smile that always cheered her up inside.

She wasn't going to tell him that right this second, what was on her mind was the fact that her kitchen never seemed so small as when she was standing beside him at the counter. He was a lot taller than she was, and his broad shoulders took up serious space. They'd decided to make cheeseburgers and fries, and she was so aware of him as he flipped their burgers in the grill pan at the stove while she sliced tomatoes.

Such a domestic cozy scene, she thought. Between being reminded of her old dreams by the window display of the bridal salon and this man helping make dinner, every now and then humming a Beatles song, Hannah felt on edge. She couldn't give in to her attraction to him for so many reasons. There was her trust level, at an all-time low. Then there was their very connection and why they'd met in the first place—a little complicated. Add in that he was her baby's doting uncle and any problems between them could mean ruining Chase and Danny's very special relationship. She wanted a loving uncle in Danny's life. And there was also the fact that Chase Dawson lived five hours away and had a whole life waiting for him there.

He was in Winston to help save the ranch. Then he'd leave. He'd visit Danny every few months, most likely, even if he'd FaceTime once a week. He wouldn't be in *her* life except peripherally.

But the main reason why she couldn't possibly fall for Chase was because she was scared spitless of the idea. Everything she'd thought was true about her ex had been a big terrible lie. That she'd been so wrong had flattened her. And all she'd endured and lost because she'd been that wrong? She'd just not take the chance again. Not when her baby son came first.

So stop telling Chase so much. Making yourself vulnerable. Just keep things impersonal. Friendly but not too *friendly.*

She set aside the fixings and got out the buns,

prepared to make small talk now that the big stuff was taken care of.

"Oh, just…this and that," she said, finally answering his question and feigning concentration of slicing open the buns.

"I might be wrong," he said, adding cheese to the burgers. "But I think I saw your friend—from the photo in the living room—at the back of the coffee shop earlier."

She inwardly sighed. How did he know? And how did he read her so well?

Talking about Jasmine would bring on the waterworks. Not the way to start a shift in her and Chase's relationship from sharing personal stuff to basic small talk.

But of course he'd noticed Jasmine, because he noticed everything. He paid attention. And he'd recognized her because he'd taken the time to look at the photo of her and Hannah in the first place and ask about it.

Just nod and start talking about the different kind of tomatoes there are. Or lettuces. Hannah could talk about burger toppings for an hour. But try as she might to focus on the juicy red tomato slices in front of her to make conversation about them, Jasmine's angry face came to mind, and a small sob escaped her.

Chase turned to her, concern on his face. "Hannah?"

She felt her shoulders slump and that familiar ache deep in her chest. "I ran into her before the announcement and it wasn't pretty," she said. So much for small talk about tomatoes. "I did see her on the other side at the coffee shop and what I'd told her was confirmed, but she left without even looking my way." She put the buns in the toaster oven. "I guess I just need to let it go, let the friendship go." But her eyes welled with tears and blinking them back didn't help.

Chase tipped her chin up and saw that she was crying and then pulled her into his arms. "Might take some people longer to come around," he said against her hair.

Why did this have to feel so good? She could stay pressed against his muscular chest forever, the strength of his arms around her so comforting. "And some may never," she said, realizing she was sunk when it came to resisting how easy it was to talk to him, to open up. "I have to accept that."

"I'm really sorry, Hannah. You've been through a lot." He tightened his hold on her for a moment, then pulled back to look at her face as if making sure she was okay. They locked gazes for a moment, and she felt so close to him that her knees began to wobble. She had to get control, command, of herself with this man. Or she'd be in big trouble.

"You okay?" he asked.

She sucked in a quick breath. "I'll be okay."

He gave her that smile again and moved back to the stove, using the spatula to take the cheeseburgers out of the pan, the cheese perfectly melted. But this time the smile comforted *and* made her nervous as heck. "I hope you have an appetite for my burgers supreme."

She couldn't help but smile herself and wiped under her eyes. "Oh yeah? What makes them so supreme?"

"Magic ingredients," he said.

She grinned, somehow feeling better. And then she was so overwhelmed by *everything* that before she could stop herself, she leaned up and kissed him on the cheek—just when he turned his head to her.

Her lips landed on his.

But instead of pulling back for all the reasons that had whizzed through her head five minutes ago, she leaned *in*.

So did Chase.

His lips were equally firm and soft. Mmmm. She could also stay *here* forever…

The timer on the homemade sweet potato fries went off, and they both took a step back.

"That was unexpected," he said, searching her eyes.

She hurried over to the oven to avoid letting

him see just how much she liked that kiss, that she wanted more. And to have something immediate to do with her hands, which she might start wringing otherwise.

"An accident," she rushed to say. "I went to kiss you on the *cheek* and you turned at that exact moment, so neither of us meant to *kiss-kiss* each other."

"Except we both did kiss-kiss each other," he pointed out, his gaze on hers. "*After* the accidental collide of lips."

She stared at him, unable to look away, goose bumps trailing up her spine. "Wow, those fries smell good," she said, slipping her hands into oven mitts and pulling out the baking tray. She was still so dazed she was surprised she didn't drop it.

"It's been some day," he said. "Highly charged. For both of us. So anything that happens isn't our fault." He smiled that smile, and all she wanted was to fling herself into his arms for another hug.

Another kiss.

But he was giving her a nice out and she had to take it.

Because falling for Chase Dawson was *not* an option.

Chapter Seven

Chase was in bed, unable to sleep at 1:17 a.m. when he heard a baby crying.

And crying.

Still crying.

He sat up, wanting to go knock on Hannah's door and ask if he could help. But things between them had been a little awkward during dinner and after, and they'd gone into their rooms and hadn't emerged at the same times. He had heard Hannah's phone ringing often, which was likely a good sign that people were calling to discuss the big revelations from Chase's announcement at the coffee shop. Maybe a call was from her old friend Jasmine.

One little kiss had hovered in the air between them over their cheeseburgers and sweet potato fries, every glance between them suddenly... charged.

Conversation over dinner had been unusual, Hannah launching into a rundown on various breeds of tomatoes, then her favorite sheep at the McCord Ranch, and what a hard worker Owen's part-time hand was. She'd kept the conversation impersonal, and he'd gone with it, wanting to make her feel comfortable with him again. And when he said he'd clean up, she practically flew to her bedroom with Danny. He'd come out of his room a few times, hoping to run into her in the kitchen or hallway. Hoping they could talk, about anything, even tomatoes.

But she hadn't or had been so purposely quiet he hadn't heard.

One kiss had done all that?

He wasn't sure if that meant he should stop thinking about the kiss, which had been short but hot, affecting *every* part of his body, or if there should be another one because clearly, there was something between them. Ignoring it would only make things more awkward. He supposed he should leave it to Hannah.

A loud shriek cut into his thoughts.

Should he offer to help? Stay put?

Dammit. The urge to help was too strong. As was the need to see Hannah. Maybe clear the air between them. Not that he knew how to make that happen.

Chase got out of bed and knocked on her door. At her slightly frantic "Come on in," he found her pacing by the window with Danny vertical against her chest, combining rocking, bouncing and rubbing the baby's back as he shrieked and kicked.

"He's inconsolable," she said, shifting him a bit. "I've changed him, I've tried to feed him. I don't know what he wants." She walked to the basket on her dresser and used her free hand to pluck out a forehead thermometer. "No fever. He's not pulling at his ears. What's wrong, Boo-Boo?" she cooed to the baby, giving him a nuzzle.

Which made Danny shriek even more. Hannah looked frazzled. And tired.

"Let me take him," he offered. "I know from my cousins' kids' birthday parties that sometimes a change in arms and scenery—like my Wyoming Cowboys T-shirt instead of your pink-and-white tank top—can do wonders for a screeching baby."

Not that Hannah didn't look delectable in that tank top. Despite the screaming baby, the sight of her had him swallowing. He had to force his eyes off her as she handed him the baby so he could focus.

Once he had Danny against his chest, the little guy almost instantly quieted down, staring at him with those uncanny similar eyes.

"You like the U of Wyoming logo, huh?" he asked the baby, glancing down at his black T-shirt with the gold silhouette of a rider, one hand with his hat in the air, on a bucking horse. "Little cowboy in the making, maybe," he added, gently swaying him in his arms. Danny stared up at him, his eyes a bit droopy but the tiny boy was fighting sleep. "Rock-a-bye, Danny, on the tree branch," he sang, no idea how the lullaby actually went. "When the wind comes, the baby will dance. When the tree breaks, the braaaannch will fall, and I will catch baaaaaby, screeching and all."

Hannah had gone from frazzled to laughing pretty quickly. "Baby soother and lullabies on the fly. I'm very impressed, Chase Dawson."

"I remembered the tune but not the words," he said with a chuckle. He looked down at Danny. "My work here is done. Fast asleep." He swayed him a bit very gently for a few moments, then headed to the bassinet. "If I can actually transfer him without waking him up, then you can be impressed."

"He transfers pretty easily."

"Oh. You should have let me think I had some

magical baby powers," he said on a grin. He laid the baby down. One little hand shot up by his head, a lip quirked, but he did not wake up.

They both waited, silent, for a few seconds.

"I owe you," she said. "I knew there was a good reason for you stay here while you're in town." She was smiling, but there was a hesitancy.

While you're in town...

He wondered why that poked at him. The idea that he'd be leaving? Saying goodbye to Hannah and Danny and Owen just when they'd become part of his life?

His reason for bursting into her room was over, and he didn't want to go back to his alone with all these thoughts and questions.

"I could go for a cup of tea, something herbal," he said. "How about you?"

Please say yes.

"But no accidental kisses over the sugar bowl or anything," she said.

He gave a solemn nod, which she returned as though they were making some sort of pact, then they headed out of her room and went down the short hallway to the kitchen.

"We should talk about the kiss, though," he said.

"Or not. It was a moment in time, that's all. I was feeling sad, you cheered me up, and physics combined with forced proximity of a narrow, small kitchen made it happen. It wouldn't have happened in the living room. We simply wouldn't have been standing *that* close together."

He smiled and took two mugs from the cabinet while Hannah filled the teakettle. "We're kissing distance again," he said, reaching for the boxes of tea.

She made a show of taking two big steps to the right. Chase laughed and chose a chamomile tea bag. "I'll have that too," she said.

"I'm not trying to make light of anything, Hannah," he said as she poured the steaming water into the mugs. "Just want to acknowledge what happened. Because it did happen. And maybe for another reason than physics and proximity."

"I know very well what that reason is," she said. "I fully admit to being attracted to you on number of levels. But I don't plan to act on it. For my own well-being. Let's leave it at that."

He gave another solemn nod as they sat down with their tea and added cream and sugar, both of them steeping the tea bags and focusing on that instead of on each other. But she was all he could think about.

"I was so stupid," she said suddenly, that same strangled sob coming from her throat. "About Kent," she added, glancing down at her tea. She wrapped her hands around the mug. "I knew he had a reputation for dating and never committing. And like a fool, I thought I was the one who would tame him." She shook her head. "For the two months we were together, we saw each other practically every night and entire weekends, so I assumed we were a couple, that we were headed somewhere."

"What was he like?" Chase found himself asking without meaning to. But he did want to know more about his twin.

"Dynamic. He was a chatterbox. He talked about anything, any subject, and started fascinating conversations. He chatted up everyone from elderly ladies sitting on their porches at night to waiters at restaurants. Always friendly, always interested in other people. It's how he reeled everyone in, made them feel like he cared."

"Then you can't blame yourself, Hannah. From what I've been piecing together, he came into the con artist business only recently or he would have had a reputation for that too. But everyone liked him, right? He got into trouble—likely very big trouble—with gambling, and he saw an opportunity to save his hide. And the more money he got control of, the more he was likely to gamble and the bigger trouble he found himself in."

Hannah nodded. "To the point that he betrayed

his own father. And me. Swindled my parents. Between the police beginning an investigation and me telling him I was pregnant, he fled. Want to know what he said when I told him?" Her face kind of crumpled, and it was all he could do not to leap out of his chair and hold her.

He wasn't sure he did want to know. But Hannah needed to tell him, and so he'd listen and do his job here. Which was to comfort her, be her friend, her shoulder.

She took a long sip of her tea. "He got the strangest look on his face. I couldn't really pin it down. Until he said, 'Poor kid.' Then he looked at me and added, 'You take care, Hannah,' and turned and walked away. He looked back once and then kept going. I was so stunned I just stood there, staring after him until he was out of my sight line. In the morning, he and his stuff were gone. That was nine months ago."

"'Poor kid'?" Chase repeated. "Because of who his father was," he said as he realized what Kent had meant. "Kent knew exactly what he was."

"Why didn't I?" she asked, turning her hazel-green eyes to him. "Why was I such a dummy?"

"You weren't, Hannah," he said, taking her hand and holding on to it. "Kent gave you no reason to doubt him, so you didn't."

"I'll never trust another man with this dumb thing," she said, slapping the left side of her chest.

He knew in time that would dissipate. But maybe with a baby—the betrayer's baby—she'd guard her heart to the point no one would break through.

He didn't want that to happen. Even if it meant helping her to find…someone else. But exploring what was between them wasn't an option.

"Is it hard on you to have me here?" he asked, finally slipping his hand from hers. "I'll go find a room somewhere if it is, Hannah. I don't want to cause you any stress."

She looked at him. "It's a little hard," she said. "For a number of reasons. But it's also great for a number of reasons. Like how you immediately calmed down Danny a few minutes ago when I couldn't. How you cleaned up from dinner. How I'm sitting here, spilling my guts, something I swore I'd stop doing so we wouldn't get closer, because you're so easy to talk to and sometimes I just burst with what's bothering me."

"Well, I'm here for you. Friends," he said, extending his hand this time.

She gave him something of a wobbly smile. "You're more like family, though. You're Danny's uncle."

"Friend of highest status," he added, waiting for her to shake on it.

She laughed and shook. Then they both drank their tea. She got up and pulled something out of the fridge and set it down on the table with two forks. She lifted off the foil. "What's left of my lemon custard pie. When I don't have anyone to talk to in the middle of the night—and when I do, apparently—I hit up the pie."

He dug his fork in and took a bite. "Mmm. So good." He took another bite.

She grinned and took a bite too. "Speaking of pie, I have good news. Between arriving home from the coffee shop announcement and midnight, I got back *seven* clients. Seven! I've got a ton of cooking and baking orders for the coming days."

He held up a palm to high five her, and she laughed as she gave his hand a good smack. "Congrats, Hannah. I'm really glad. You'll likely attract new clients, as well, from word of mouth." He held up his mug in a toast.

"I've never been so happy for gossip," she said, clinking. "I'll have to figure out a childcare solution, though, look into part-time sitters."

A very good idea presented itself. "You're looking at your childcare solution while I'm in town. It's a win-win. You can cook your heart out without worrying about anything in regard to Danny, and I get to spend some real time with my little cowboy-nephew."

Her eyes widened. "Huh. But won't you need to spend a lot of time at the ranch?"

"A lot of what I'm doing there is structural and reorganizing. I can easily do that during Danny's naps. And when I need to do some hard physical labor like muck out stalls and rearrange the barns, Danny can hang out in his stroller batting at his mobile. I can sing him more badly reworded songs."

Hannah laughed. "You sure about this?"

"Very," he said. "I told you—that Danny is my nephew means something to me. It means a lot."

She reached a hand over and squeezed his, and he wanted to just hold that hand and sit there and have another bite of her homemade pie and sip his tea and take in how lovely she was, how nice this was. But he'd respect the boundaries she'd put in place.

They were friends—of high status, but *friends*.

But things *had* changed between them, try as they would to ignore the fact. Chase couldn't ignore it the way Hannah planned to. But he was supposed to be aboveboard in all ways so that he could help her regain her trust in people.

And so he would.

* * *

The next morning, Chase and Owen mucked out the sheep pen side by side, Danny across the aisle in his stroller. Chase had been at the ranch since 7:00 a.m. and had seen Owen coming and going, riding fences, stopping to make repairs, leading the cattle out to a different pasture. Then Owen had grabbed a rake and joined him in the barn. Chase could handle the sheep pen on his own, but he sensed Owen wanted to work beside him, that he wanted to talk and would when he was ready. For the past fifteen minutes, Owen hadn't said a word.

Suddenly, he stopped and rested his weight on the handle of the rake. "I got a call from a former friend—a rancher Kent swindled. He said if I could walk away from one of my own newborn twins that I'm capable of any malfeasance." He let out a breath and turned to look at Danny. "My legs nearly gave out. That's how bad it cut me to the core."

Dammit. "I'm sorry." He laid a hand on Owen's shoulder, the man turning to him with a thankful nod.

"I guess that's just the way it's going to be. Some people will believe I was involved, that I'm hiding a fortune—made off their money— in an offshore account. But I'll tell you, coming off a call like that and seeing Danny helps like nothing else could."

Chase smiled. "I know what you mean."

Owen leaned the rake against the stall, peeled off his gloves, washed his hands at the sink at the end of the barn, and then went over to Danny's stroller and picked him up, holding him close. "Thank God for you, Danny." He brought him over to where Chase was standing. "And you, Chase. I was counting my blessings that you came to seek me out. And here you are, helping to save the ranch, turning things around for me with the townspeople. I stand here with you and Danny and suddenly that call can't get to me, you know?"

Chase swallowed around the lump that suddenly formed in this throat. He didn't know what to say so again put his hand on Owen's shoulder for a moment, letting the man know he appreciated that.

"Counting my blessings is what it's about," Owen said. "How to stay sane right now."

"You have a good attitude."

Owen gave an appreciative nod and returned Danny to his stroller, caressing the baby's capped head, then he came back over and pulled out his phone and swiped through his photos, going back a ways. "I have the sweetest photo of Hannah and

Danny I'll send you." He kept swiping, then froze on a photo, a selfie from the looks of it, of himself and a redheaded woman about his age. Owen's face fell and his shoulders slumped.

"Who's that?" Chase asked gently, his gaze on the photo.

Owen startled and quickly swiped on. "Just someone I used to know."

Someone I used to know. An ex-girlfriend? Someone who clearly still had a hold on him. Chase wondered what happened. Fallout from the Kent debacle?

"I need to check on something," Owen suddenly said and walked away, forgetting all about that "sweet photo of Hannah and Danny."

Whatever had happened between him and the redhead, it had done a number on Owen.

Chase finished mucking out the pen, the manual labor feeling good on his muscles. He was about to grab some fresh hay when he heard a very familiar voice call out, "Where's my darling boy?"

Hannah.

She came into the barn, dressed for ranch work and beelined for Danny, turning to Chase. "I ran into Owen on my way here. He sure didn't look happy. Everything okay between you two?" She scooped up Danny and twirled him around, then settled the sleepy boy back in the stroller.

"We had a great talk, actually," he said. "He was going to show me a photo of you and Danny, but he came upon a pic of himself and a redheaded woman, and his whole demeanor changed. Said she was someone he used to know."

"Someone he used to *date*. Her name is Tina Wexler. They were newly seeing each other when Kent's cons came to light."

"Ah, she broke up with him over it?"

"Actually, *he* broke up with *her*. He told her he couldn't drag her down with him, that the whole town hated him and turned against him, and they'd shun her too. She's a Realtor, and he was afraid she'd lose all her customers. So he stopped seeing her. When he told me all this, I tried to tell him to let her make that decision for herself, but he clammed up and said he'd prefer not to discuss it anymore."

"Now that things are changing, maybe there's a second chance for them."

Hannah smiled. "I hope so. She's a lovely person."

"Maybe we could help them along, somehow," Chase said, grabbing some hay and spreading it out in the pen. Or at least put them in the same place at the same time?"

Hannah turned to him with a grin before grabbing a bunch of hay. "He cooks, he babysits, he sings half-made-up lullabies—and he match-makes!"

He loved seeing her smile. "Am I being a busy-body, as my mother used to call people who med-dled in others' lives?"

"In a good way in this situation," she said. "Owen's had a really rough time these past many months. And you're a bright spot, but it's likely unnerving for him too. He doesn't know if you'll accept it or what will happen between you two—if you'll get close, if you'll just go home once you got the ranch back on its feet. A special lady in his life would do wonders for him."

Huh. He hadn't thought about how he might be affecting Owen. If the man was unsettled about what their relationship would be—if any.

Thing was, Chase didn't know.

He had a good feeling about Owen; he liked the man. But there was still no emotional con-nection for Chase. And Chase wondered if he just wasn't capable of feeling it. Maybe he'd just gone too long without a father. Maybe the void was just too deep.

What had Chase's ex-girlfriend said when she'd broken up with him? *You're just...distant*.

Maybe it was better that Hannah was drawing

the line between them. *Distant* wouldn't help her regain her trust.

But instead of feeling better on that front, he just felt...on his own.

Chapter Eight

Something seemed different about Chase after their conversation in the barn. He'd gotten quiet, unusual for him. She'd helped him finish the sheep pen and wanted to stay longer to find out if something was bothering him, but she was meeting her mother at her apartment at 1:00 p.m. for a marathon cooking session. Bettina had the afternoon off and was excited to be her assistant.

She'd had to say goodbye to Danny—again—but she knew her son was in good hands with Chase.

Part of her wished she could feel that way too. Just let herself go with what had become so clear:

that Chase Dawson was a really good guy. Dependable. Honest. Helpful. Compassionate. He'd shown her those traits over and over.

True to his word, Chase had plucked Danny from his bassinet at first peep at five thirty this morning and had been on uncle-sitter duty ever since. While Hannah fulfilled one big order for a diabetic client and then pored over her recipe book and made ingredient lists for the others, Chase had poured her two cups of coffee, brought her over a bowl of green and red grapes, put Danny down for his morning nap, and actually started folding Danny's laundry that she'd done this morning. She'd told him she'd take care of that, but he tossed her a cheerful "no problem," and continued making neat stacks of onesies and fleece pj's and socks. Which he'd put away in Danny's dresser. Then he'd sat on the sofa with his laptop, going over what looked like McCord Ranch ledgers and taking copious notes. She'd offered to make him breakfast, but he said he'd make himself an omelet in a little while.

He was a miracle.

Then he'd gone to the ranch to help out there, and when she'd arrived to put in a couple hours and see Danny, she'd realized she'd missed Chase too.

Which didn't sit well with her. Fall for a guy

and *wham*—before you could blink or compre-
hend what had happened to your life, he was gone
with your heart and your trust. Good guys could
lose interest just like the players. Get bored. Fall
for someone else.

Was she making excuses? Coming up with anything to avoid giving in to her attraction to Chase?
Probably. But she sure felt on steadier ground that
way.

Now, Hannah was in her kitchen, her mother
ready in her thirty-year-old apron, a gift from
Hannah's late grandmother. On her way home
from the ranch, Hannah had stopped off in the
grocery store to buy the ingredients she didn't
have on hand for the two rush orders she'd gotten
last night. One was a week's worth of easy-to-reheat kid-friendly dinners, "two different homemade mac and cheese options, please" and at least
one "healthy chicken nuggets"; the other was for
three pies for a book club group with a different pastry focus each month. Every time Hannah baked pies for clients, she made a few extra
for herself.

Now she wondered what Chase Dawson's favorite kind of pie was. *Because he's staying here*,
she rationalized.

While her mother washed her hands at the sink,
Hannah sent the man in question a quick text:

Favorite kind of pie?

He answered right away, as he always did.

I could have pumpkin pie all day, every day, year-round. Also love chocolate pudding pie, childhood fave. Pecan too. Strange thing about me: fruit pie—eh. Oh, and I like those little pies—tarts?

Hannah laughed. She loved tarts too. And every kind of fruit pie, but hey, they couldn't have *everything* in common. But chocolate pudding pie? Pumpkin? Oh yeah. And pecan was on her top five list.

"Someone's making you smile and laugh?" her mother said, eyeing her phone screen and edging closer. "Wrap that person up and keep 'em close."

Hannah bit her lip and slid her phone into her apron pocket. "I don't know about that, Mom. Chase was just telling me his favorite kind of pie since I want to make extras."

"What don't you know about that?" Bettina asked. "If I may be so nosy."

"He's…complicated, don't you think?"

"Actually, I think he's pretty great, Hannah. I barely know him, of course, but I've seen him in action. He took a hopeless situation and turned it around. Which is also what he's doing with the McCord Ranch. He's said lovely things I heard with my own ears. And the way he is with Danny? Warms a granny's heart."

Hannah inwardly sighed, Chase's handsome face floating into her mind. *He folds laundry too. And puts it away.* "Yeah, mine too. That's the problem."

"He's not Kent, honey. That's what that announcement was all about, right?"

Hannah raised an eyebrow. "He's still scary, though."

"It's always scary to put yourself at risk in any situation. But you've always gone after your dreams, Hannah. That's who you are. You're already inching toward him. It's the reason you invited him to stay here."

Hannah froze for a second. Huh. That was true. She was inching. Closer and closer.

"When you're ready, you'll know," her mother added, giving her a pat on the shoulder.

"How do you always manage to make me feel better?" Hannah asked.

"Because I love you and want you to be happy—on your terms."

Hannah felt her eyes mist, and she put down her wooden spoon and grabbed her mom into a hug. "I don't know what I'd do without you."

"You can bake a pie for me and Dad, how about that? I'll even help with that one. I'm thinking key lime."

Hannah smiled. Their mutual favorite. "Done."

They got to work, the conversation turning to a funny story from the bank this morning, and then they were concentrating on the recipes and listening to music. Hannah tried to put Chase out of her mind as she whipped up his pumpkin pie, then two chocolate pudding tarts and one pecan pie. She put her heart and soul into those bakes, imagining him feeding her a bite…

Whoa. Back to reality.

Once the pies were in the oven, they got started on the weekly meal order. Hannah made an extra crock of mac and cheese for her and Chase, wondering if she should add bacon.

"I think it's very nice how you take him into consideration," Bettina said. "You're an excellent host."

"Well, you should have seen him in action this morning. He folded Danny's laundry into neat stacks. Then put it all away. I know he offered to watch Danny while I work, but I didn't expect such royal treatment. He deserves mac and cheese with bacon. And three pies and a tart."

"Like I said, Hannah, *inching*. And I'm very

happy about that. You're letting yourself trust him."

Hannah thought about that. "The beginning stages, anyway. He's proven himself as someone I can count on. Plus I like how he is with Owen and what he's doing there. He's setting his aside his own life to help Owen when he doesn't even know how he feels about the man. Chase is just a good person."

He'd even noticed how Owen had stopped on the photo of himself and Tina, his ex-girlfriend, that something was bothering Owen about it. Chase *saw* because he cared. Cared about people in general. And Owen specifically. Her mother had been right about Chase feeling more than he realized when it came to his father. Maybe he just wasn't ready to realize.

Like Hannah.

"Agreed," Bettina said, opening the dishwasher and putting in the mixing bowls. "I think he probably does know how he feels about Owen. But you want to talk about scary stuff? Developing a relationship at age twenty-eight with the father you never knew—not even a name? Of course he's keeping a distance. Same as you are with Chase. You two have a lot more in common than you might realize."

Huh again. Hannah hadn't thought of that.

She wondered what he and Danny were up to. Was Chase showing his nephew the sheep? Teaching him how to baaa? She smiled at the thought. He was probably doing exactly that.

With Danny elsewhere, she thought she'd be constantly looking over her shoulder in the apartment, expecting to see her baby in his swing or to hear him cry out from his nap. But she really had been able to concentrate on her work. Because she *did* trust Chase.

Her mother, as usual, was right. But trusting him made the thought of giving in to her attraction all the more scary.

At seven thirty that night, Chase sat on the sofa in Hannah's living room, three small slices of pie before him. That she'd gone to the trouble of baking his favorites when she'd had pies to make for clients had touched him.

"As if this even comes close to paying you back for babysitting Danny today," she said, bringing over a tray of steaming coffee mugs, cream and sugar. She sat down next to him, a plate of tiny samples of the pies in front of her too. Small place, small sofa—which meant Hannah was just inches from him, their thighs almost touching. He could smell her shampoo, mingling with the scents of the pie. She'd changed into a long tank top and yoga pants, had her hair loose past her shoulders instead of the ponytail she'd worn earlier, and looked unbearably sexy.

"No payback, not even a thank you is necessary," he said, adding cream and sugar to his coffee. "It's my pleasure, seriously. Danny is a hoot. Besides, he sleeps a lot."

"He is a good napper. I got lucky there."

"Owen was happy to have him at the ranch all day," Chase said. "He kept finding excuses to come ask me a question just so he could pick up Danny." That the man adored his grandson was an understatement.

"Oh—that reminds me," she said. "While I was cooking and baking today, I was wracking my brain for ways to get Owen and his ex-girlfriend in the same place at the same time. Want to hear my grand plan? It's iffy but will at least get them talking." She cut into the pecan pie and took a bite. "Mmm, so good—if I do say so myself."

Chase took a bite of the pecan too. "Delicious. Now I have to try the other two." He cut two big bites of the chocolate pudding and pumpkin and ate them together, which made Hannah laugh. "Absolutely scrumptious."

"Why, thank you," she said with a grin.

"So let's hear your plan for Owen and his ex," he said, sipping his coffee.

"Well, about a week ago, Owen mentioned that he was considering adopting a dog, a pet and helper out in the pastures with the cattle and sheep. I remember thinking, *I will take you to the animal shelter myself if it means you'll have a friendly, loyal companion that will make you smile.* But he seemed in no great rush. And this afternoon, when I was at the grocery store, I happened to spot a notice on the community bulletin board about two border collies who are up for adoption—and guess whose ad it was? Tina's! She's fostering the dogs and looking to find a great home for them. We just have to get Owen over to Tina's to see the dogs without him first knowing it's her house."

Chase gobbled up two more bites of mixed pies. "It's a great plan, but won't he recognize the address since they dated?"

"She was new to town when they first started seeing each other and was staying with her cousin until she could find a place of her own, and it's been nine months, so I'm sure the address is that new home. I'll tell Owen about the ad I saw, ask him if he wants to go see the dogs, and hopefully he'll say yes."

"So how do you think it'll go, though?" Chase asked. "I mean, it could be very awkward for both of them. She could be in a serious relationship for all we know."

She bit her lip. "I know. I'm a little unsure about sticking my nose in their business. But sometimes people could use a little nudge."

That was the truth. Wasn't he trying to nudge Hannah toward letting her guard down?

"If it's not meant to be, fine," she said. "Owen's been through so much. And he's so good to me and Danny. I just want him to be *happier*."

Chase nodded. He felt for the man too. Owen's entire life had been filled with traumatic experiences, from what happened to him at seventeen. To losing his wife—and so young. To Kent destroying the ranch. To Owen breaking his own heart to save Tina's standing in town.

And here was long-lost son, maybe adding more stress in the man's life. With Chase's standoffishness when it came to Owen, he knew he likely was a big question mark for the man. Would Chase stay? Would he embrace their relationship? Would he want to get closer? Owen had to be wondering all that.

"I'm in," Chase said with a firm nod.

Hannah smiled and took a bite of her chocolate pudding tart. "I'm glad you're a romantic."

Chase raised an eyebrow. "Me? Nah. I'm so not a romantic that my last girlfriend told me I was difficult to get to know. And distant. She said if I didn't know if she was the one after three months of dating, she wasn't."

He hadn't meant to say all that. Hannah had a way of making him talk. *Share.*

"Was she?" Hannah asked.

"I liked her. She had a great sense of humor and loved horses. But I never thought about the future when it came to her."

"So I guess she was right."

He nodded. "Yeah, she was." He opened his mouth to say what was on his mind, then clamped his lips shut. What was he doing? They were supposed to be arm's length, not getting closer. But talking to Hannah was just too easy, too comfortable. He never opened up this way with anyone.

"But," he started, and again stopped talking and filled his mouth with pecan pie instead.

"But what?" she asked, tilting her head, her blond hair falling to the side, revealing her neck.

She reached over and topped his hand with hers, her soft, warm skin sending delicious chills up his arms, up his spine. That was all it took from Hannah. A touch on his hand.

He sipped his coffee as a memory rushed into his head. "The night my mother died, I woke up in the middle of the night feeling like hell. I realized how alone I was in the world. I had my cousins,

but no immediate family. No relationship. Just…
me. Not that I want a relationship that isn't working. Guess I finally had to face that being a lone
ranger, like Owen, has its drawbacks."

He suddenly felt those soft, warm hands of hers
on either side of his face. He turned toward her,
and she kissed him. On the lips.

Unexpected.

And before he could think or process, he
wrapped her in his arms and kissed her back.

But I don't even know if I'm capable of a seri-
ous relationship. I've never had one. I've dated
a lot of women. No one's ever been the one. And
it's probably me and not them. When something
carves out a chasm in your life and keeps you
unsure and unsettled, you don't gravitate toward
people, toward handing out your heart. You go
inward. Alone.

But he didn't say any of this. First of all, it
was how Hannah was feeling these days—these
months. Almost a year. And his job here was to
help her out of it.

He didn't need to reinforce that he'd been holding back from love and relationships and commit-
ments his entire life.

She deepened the kiss, and he was losing track
of his thoughts. He processed only her—the delicious scent of her shampoo and soap, how silky

her blond hair felt against his neck and arms. How soft her lips were. The way the zipper of his jeans was feeling very, very tight.

"Hannah, I thought you said there would be no more kisses," he whispered, wanting to give her an out, snap her back to reality.

"I want this," she whispered back, holding his gaze for a moment before straddling him and kissing his neck.

Whoa. She was a woman who went after what she wanted too.

He was a goner then, unable to form another thought. He picked her up and carried her into the guest room, gently closing the door with his foot. With an eye on the baby monitor on his dresser, he gave a quick prayer that Danny wouldn't wake up for a while.

He definitely did not want to be interrupted from this.

Such a good kisser, Hannah thought, Chase's mouth possessive on hers en route to the bed. She had his shirt off in two seconds, letting it drop to the floor. Oh my—his chest. Muscled perfection. Just a bit of sexy hair running in a line down the center to the waistband of his jeans. Which she wanted off too.

She was aware she was playing with the ole

fire, that she could get terribly burned, but her desire for Chase Dawson was so powerful that she decided to just go with it, let herself have this… release. There was no resisting him tonight.

Instead of inching, she would take this giant step forward.

He leaned up and peeled off her tank top, his gaze landing on her white lace cotton bra. He looked at her as though she were the most beautiful woman he'd ever seen, which she appreciated. She'd just had a baby three months ago, and her body was…jiggly. But the way he took her in, the heat in his blue eyes, she felt very sexy instead of squishy. She wanted her yoga pants off *now* and so she peeled them off herself, glad she'd worn the white lacy underwear today. Usually she went for very functional, but with the restored and new clients, she'd felt so empowered and had celebrated by dolling up just for herself.

Having no idea someone else would see.

He kissed her deeply as he unsnapped his jeans, then pulled back to take them off, and she got her first glimpse of his tall, muscular body. She swallowed, a wave of sensation rocking her from deep inside. Their bare legs intermingled, goose bumps trailing up and down her calves, behind her knees. His mouth was back on hers, and she felt him reaching up with his left hand on the bedside table. She opened her eyes—he was fumbling in his wallet.

"Success," he whispered with a smile, his right hand cupping her face. "It's been a long time for me, but the old advice is hard to part with. Always keep a condom in your wallet."

"Even I have one. And I thought I'd never be having sex *again*."

He laughed and kissed her, a hand roaming to her back to unhook her bra. He took it off, and then his hands and mouth were everywhere, making her arch and let out moans she barely knew were from her. He went lower, kissing his way down her stomach and inched down her underwear, and within seconds her eyes closed and her back arched again as waves of pleasure unfurled inside her. Then he kissed his way back up her stomach to her cleavage, lingering on each breast before finding her mouth.

Her hand found its way down to his incredibly sexy black boxer briefs and slid inside. His gasp made her smile, her toes curling.

And then she heard the tearing of the condom wrapper and moments later, he was poised over her, looking at her again, this time with desire tinged with tenderness.

I love you, she thought in the far recesses of her mind.

And then she'd lost all ability to think at all as she felt his first thrust, her nails digging into his back.

Chapter Nine

Chase awoke to the sound of Hannah singing a familiar lullaby. Eyes still closed, he reached over to curl up beside her, but he was alone in bed. His eyes popped open—he was facing the baby monitor—where the singing was coming from.

The sun filtered in through the curtains, which meant it was morning, but had Chase actually slept the whole night? He must have. He hadn't heard Danny wake up—and he usually cried out twice. Chase's ears had gotten sensitive to those little baby sounds; clearly he'd slept hard and he knew exactly why that was.

Chase smiled, clasping his arms behind his

head as he remembered every delicious detail of his time in bed with Hannah. That she'd let last night happen meant something had changed for her. She trusted him.

The nursery monitor turned quiet. Hmm, perhaps she would put Danny in the playpen, sneak back to his room and slide into bed with him for just a few minutes. Even a quick spooning or "good morning" whispered between kisses. He waited, but she never did come back. He got out of bed and took a quick shower, then headed toward her voice, coming from the kitchen.

Danny was in his baby swing, and Hannah was brewing coffee.

"A very good morning to you," he said, aware he had a goofy smile on his face.

The moment she looked at him, he knew there would be no dashing back to bed for a quick repeat. *Awkward* had returned.

"Look, Chase, um," she began, turning away to reach for two mugs. "I, um…"

"Hey," he said gently. "You don't have to say anything. I can read you. You're not sure last night should have happened."

"I know it shouldn't have," she said in a rush, then winced. "Sorry. I'm just…" She turned away again and bit her lip.

"Hannah, it's okay. I'll tell you this, though.

I'm *glad* last night happened. Every second of it. But for you, if last night was last night and today is a new day, that's fine. I'm here for you. Above all else, I'm your friend."

She looked at him then, her expression softening, her shoulders relaxing. She seemed about to say something but must have thought better of it and poured their coffees instead. "I don't have any orders to start on till this afternoon, so I'm going to take Danny over to the ranch. I can talk to Owen about the dogs."

The dogs. For a moment he couldn't remember what she was talking about, since his brain was caught on the distance she was putting between them while he was trying to hold on to how close he'd felt to her last night. But then it came to him. Owen's ex was fostering two dogs, and Owen had expressed interest in adopting. A way to get the two in the same place at the same time. And,let romance take its course.

But it didn't always. It certainly wasn't for him and Hannah.

Of course, Chase *had* to be wonderful, Hannah thought as she drove through the gates of the McCord Ranch.

She, on other hand, had been anything but. She'd wanted to apologize before she'd left for how she'd acted—so strained and awkward and "last night shouldn't have happened." Imagine if he'd said that to her—despite her misgivings about pursuing a romantic relationship with him, she would have been hurt. But he'd sipped his coffee and toasted a bagel, picking up Danny and blowing raspberries on his belly while he waited for the toaster oven to ping. And as he spread cream cheese, he kept up a running commentary to Danny about the McCord Ranch and which grasses the sheep and cattle preferred and that he was going to walk the fence line today in the near pastures and see what needed repairing. Between bites of bagel, he told Danny they were lucky Owen had a good, small herd left.

Hannah's eyes had widened when she realized Chase would be at the ranch when she'd be there, which of course should not be a surprise. Working at the ranch was the whole reason he was still in Winston. But getting over Chase while *seeing* him—his six feet three of muscular cowboy and all-around great guy—was going to be impossible. Especially after the incredible sex they'd had.

Last night, when a cry from Danny gave her the excuse to leave his warm bed, she'd found herself practically running to her room. *Sorry, but I'm scared to death of you*, she'd thought, taking a last look at him lying there, the blanket up to his amazing pecs.

Scared because of what she'd been thinking when she'd been so lost in a haze of pleasure. *I love you.* It had come bursting out of her heart, and thank heavens she hadn't actually *said it*.

Hannah couldn't afford to love anyone, especially Chase Dawson. The ties that bound them were too deep and intense and complicated. Complicated didn't begin to cover the fact that she had a history—and a baby!—with the identical twin he never knew existed until very recently.

Even if last night, everything had felt so easy and free and simple. Attraction. Lust. Sex.

Stop thinking about it, she ordered herself as she parked her car by the barns and then unlatched Danny from his car seat. Today was sweeping and mopping day in the barns, and the physical work was exactly what she needed this morning. As she put Danny in his stroller and settled him over by the corner, Hannah grabbed the broom and got to work.

She figured the mindlessness would help clear her mind, be almost zen-like, but instead, all she could think of was Chase. How incredibly hot last night had been. He'd been so attentive, whispering the sweetest somethings in her ear about how beautiful she was, how sexy. She'd *loved* last night. She didn't regret it—even if she knew she couldn't let it happen again. She felt so much for Chase, and it was all stuffed down just under the surface where she could control it, keep a lid on it. If she gave into it, the way she had physically last night, she'd be lost to herself. Her heart would belong to Chase when she needed it firmly in her chest and with Danny. Chase wasn't going to be here in Winston for very long, anyway.

"There's my sweet grandbaby," came Owen's voice. She smiled at him as he made his way over to Danny, plucking him from the stroller and carrying him around, hoisting him high and then bringing him down low, causing Danny to burst out with his adorable laughter.

"I'll never understand how such a big sound comes from such a tiny body," Owen said with a grin. He blew a raspberry on Danny's belly, as Chase had this morning, earning more laughter.

"Oh, Owen," she began, trying to inject some lightness into her voice. "At the grocery store yesterday, I saw a post on the bulletin board about two border collies up for adoption. There was a photo too—they were beyond cute and looked very smart." She pulled out her phone and held up the photo she'd taken of the ad. Thankfully, no name was mentioned. There was just a cell phone number to call or text.

Owen tilted his head and stared at the photo. "Border collies, huh. Just what I had in mind. I was thinking *one* dog, though. We barely need even one for help in the fields as it is. But they sure are beauts," he added, still looking at the photo.

Yes!

"How about we go over tonight and meet them?" she said. "I think a dog would bring great cheer to the McCord Ranch."

"Yeah, I think you're right. I've always wanted a dog, and for this or that reason it never worked out. My late wife was allergic. And Kent didn't like dogs. He was snapped at by a Chihuahua as a kid, and that was that for him."

"He didn't tell me that story," Hannah said. Ever since he fled town, she wondered about all he *had* told her. What was true and what wasn't. Everything always sounded so plausible.

"Well, if he had brought it up, he would have turned that Chihuahua into a big, scary junkyard dog."

Hanna smiled. "Probably.

Owen shook his head. "Look at us. Talking about you-know-who and actually smiling. Maybe we're making progress, Hannah."

Huh. "I think you're right."

Was it Chase Dawson's influence? Spreading his own good cheer in her and Owen's lives? Had last night loosened her up a little? She wouldn't have thought so this morning from her reaction to seeing him in the kitchen. But maybe he'd gotten through just a little.

She smiled again.

Owen gave a firm nod. "Yeah, let's go see those pups. I've always loved border collies. Ever since I was a kid. I volunteered at the animal shelter in Bear Ridge, washing bowls and folding doggie blankets. When I got older I was allowed to walk the dogs, and there was this one, a border collie I had my heart set on adopting but my parents didn't like dogs. It was a like a knife to the heart when someone adopted that pooch, even though I was happy he was getting a home."

"Aww," she said. "That ad sounds meant to be. Why don't I text the foster mom?"

"Go right ahead," he said. "How's six thirty for you?"

"Great," she said, pulling out her phone.

A rancher friend is interested in adopting a border collie. Could we come tonight to see the dogs? Around 6:30 if that works for you?

She was about to pocket her phone when it pinged. "Hey, she responded! Six thirty is good for her," Hannah said. "And the address isn't too far from here. We'll pick you up. Chase and Danny and me."

He brightened even more at the idea of having company. Owen had been a solitary figure for way too long.

She tried to keep her smile from taking over her entire face. Starting at 6:30 tonight, Owen McCord might be *inching* his way back to his former love.

Of course, the whole plan could be a disaster. But on the chance that something good would come from it, Hannah thought it was well worth trying.

After texting Chase the good news, Hannah stopped at the grocery store at the far end of Main Street to pick up avocados and chili peppers for the five-course vegan Mexican feast she'd be making tomorrow for a couple's anniversary dinner. Several people came over to say hello and comment on Chase's big reveal and how exciting it had been to have the chief of police talk about fingerprints and DNA like a *Law and Order* episode. What a relief it was to go grocery shopping without keeping her head down, getting in and getting out, and instead letting herself enjoy the experience and be inspired with new recipe ideas.

"Well, I guess you were telling the truth about

Kent having an identical twin he never knew about," a familiar voice said.

Hannah looked up from where she stood by the bin of chili peppers. Jasmine was focused on the asparagus selection, not even looking at Hannah, but it was definitely her old friend who'd spoken.

"Yes," Hannah said, turning to face her. "I was as shocked as everyone else."

Jasmine still wasn't looking at her. Most people wouldn't ignore a baby—and in this case, Danny was wide awake in his stroller right between where the two women were standing—but Jasmine didn't even glance at Danny. Hannah's chest felt tight, and annoying tears misted her eyes. This was her oldest friend. Her best friend since second grade. They'd shared everything, confided in each other, went through all their firsts together.

But Hannah would miss Jasmine's wedding because she wouldn't be invited in the first place. A memory floated through her mind of her and Jasmine as seventh graders, passing a bridal shop in town that no longer existed. Jasmine had stopped to look in the window at the three wedding gowns on mannequins and said when she got married, she'd wear a movie-star-type white satiny gown from the 1940s paired with fancy white cowboy boots, and her wedding would be at a dude ranch, twinkling lights strung in the trees. She and her beloved would ride off on white horses. Fitting since Jasmine was a traveling horse groomer. It had been Hannah who'd said she'd wanted the traditional big poufy dress and veil, a church ceremony, and a huge party with a first dance with her dad and a giant wedding cake.

"Will you be wearing white cowboy boots for the big day?" Hannah dared to ask with a gentle smile.

Please respond. Please let's be friends again. Just a start.

Jasmine finally turned to her and threw the asparagus she held back down. "Just because you weren't lying about the twin thing doesn't mean you didn't know Kent was a lying con man. I'm barely *having* a wedding thanks to him. First of all, the ceremony is in my parents' backyard instead of the Winston Dude Ranch like I'd planned. Second of all, we're having a simple buffet instead of a sit-down meal. Just what I always wanted to serve at my wedding—a bunch of appetizers." Her brown eyes were glinting with anger. She shook her head and stared down at the ground, then back up. "My cousin, a budding photographer, is gifting me her services but she can barely focus a camera."

Oh, Jasmine, Hannah thought. *I am so sorry.* Her friend had been dreaming of her wedding day since she was in middle school—when she and her fiancé had actually starting dating. She'd made mood boards and had Pinterest and Instagram accounts devoted to her ideas of the perfect dude ranch wedding. Hannah could understand why a backyard, appetizers and a not great photographer wouldn't live up to the dream.

Jasmine's eyes misted with tears. "My mom tells me to count my blessings and I try, you know? But I'm so damned angry. I *had* the money. Michael and I have been saving up for the wedding for *two* years."

Now Hannah's eyes filled with tears. "I know." She'd said she was sorry so many times, and she knew it was the last thing Jasmine wanted to hear.

"And I know I sound like a brat, Hannah. I'm lucky I have the love of my life and honestly, I'd marry him in a dirt hut. But to lose our money to a *con man*—that's what I can't get over. That I can't afford anything I want because someone stole our savings. And worse—because we actually *handed over* our account, expecting that liar to invest safely." She shook her head.

Hannah dared to reach out a hand to Jasmine's arm. Her old friend didn't pull away or snarl at her. A very good sign.

An idea came to her. Hmm…

"Jasmine, I'm thinking out loud here. But what

if you had the wedding at the McCord Ranch? The setting is beautiful. With a white tent and white lights strung in the trees nearby, you'd have a few of the mountains. And I could cater a sit-down meal—at no expense to you. A caterer I used to work for a few years back would let me borrow tables and chairs and flatware and glasses. The only true expense would be flowers and a better photographer."

For a moment, Jasmine's expression seemed to be softening, but then it turned stony again. "So I should get married at your rat bastard ex's ranch? Right, Hannah."

With that, she stalked off.

"Jasmine, please wait," Hannah called after her. "It's not the same ranch anymore. It's something completely different now." She wished Jasmine would turn around so she could explain what she meant, how the very sentiment was everything to Owen and gave him the wherewithal to keep the ranch from going under completely.

Months ago, Owen had said: *Enough. I'm going to try to save the ranch. It won't be the same, but that's good because it won't be the ranch Kent destroyed. It'll be something new.* Because of that and the hard work both of them had put in at the ranch, Hannah had long stopped associating the place with Kent; it was all Owen to her. She hadn't thought Jasmine would tie it back with Kent at this point.

Something old, something new, something borrowed, something blue, she thought miserably. Maybe she shouldn't have suggested the ranch at all. But to her, the ranch was all those things: old, new, borrowed and blue. And it was beautiful. The land was the land, the mountains were the mountains. They still had that.

But Jasmine just kept walking—right out the door of the grocery store, leaving behind her cart, which only had a few items in it. A sack of Granny Smith apples. A jar of mayonnaise. A loaf of sourdough bread. Just as a memory was about to float through her mind, of Jasmine having a green apple every day at lunch as they were growing up, all her sandwiches on her beloved sourdough bread, made by her mom, who was gone now, Hannah heard whispering.

She inwardly groaned and looked to her left. Beth Lawonski, who worked in the library, and Christine Palmer, a major gossip, were staring—and definitely whispering.

Hannah put back the chili peppers. She just wanted to get out of here. She'd just come back tomorrow, early, before the store got crowded.

"I think Jasmine would take her up on that," she heard Beth say.

"Me too," Christine whispered.

"And it's ridiculous that Jasmine thinks Hannah knew Kent was a criminal. I don't think she did. Her own parents lost most of their savings."

"Right?" Beth said.

On one hand, she hated being gossiped about. But at least they were on her side.

She wheeled Danny's stroller out the door, her heart so heavy. Would she have to give up on Jasmine and any hope of restarting their friendship? From this latest interaction, the answer was yes. Nine months hadn't changed anything. Chase's announcement hadn't changed anything. If Jasmine missed their friendship, there was no indication, just anger and resentment.

Outside, the breezy April air was refreshing on her heated face. She stood in the bright sunshine for a moment, then turned to head for her car.

"If it isn't my favorite baby," a familiar male voice called.

Hannah's shoulders sagged with relief. Chase.

He came loping across the street, his smile lighting up his handsome face. He was exactly what she needed right now. "Hey," he said, looking at her with concern as he joined her on the sidewalk. "What's wrong?"

"I ran into Jasmine just now—inside," she explained. "She said just because I wasn't lying about you being Kent's identical twin doesn't mean I didn't know he was a con man. She also said she was barely having a wedding thanks to him." She let out a breath, a rush of sadness in her chest. "So I suggested the McCord Ranch as a free venue and offered to cater a sit-down meal, but she didn't take the idea of marrying at my 'rat bastard ex's ranch.'" She sighed hard. "I shouldn't have offered it anyway without asking Owen first, but I know he'd be all for it."

He took her hand and held it. "Well, maybe she just needs to let what you offered percolate. She just might call you later and say yes, and it could be a fresh start for you two."

Hannah gave a small shrug. "I won't hold my breath. But I hope so."

"Treat to you an ice cream?" he said, taking the stroller. "I have a craving for mint chocolate chip."

"That's my favorite flavor," she said with a smile. "I might even need a double scoop." Chase and ice cream were exactly what she needed right now. She wrapped her arm around his before she even realized what she was doing.

Laying claim, almost.

Even though she'd relinquished that claim this morning.

She glanced at him, this beautiful man, inside and out, his attention focused on Danny in his stroller. Right now, Chase was making exaggerated faces at the baby.

"And just think, in a little while, we might be bringing a couple back together," he said, taking the stroller and pushing it up the sidewalk. "And getting a dog a great home."

With what just happened, she'd forgotten all about their 6:30 appointment with Tina.

But of course, he remembered. Because you could count on Chase.

"What do you think, Danny?" he said, leaning around the stroller to peer at him from the side. "Your grandpop might be a lot smilier after tonight. Then again, he's all smiles when you're around, isn't he?" He gave the baby's hair a gentle ruffle, then continued on.

Oh, Chase, she thought. *If only you were the silent type and uncomfortable around babies. Why do you have to be so...perfect for me?*

And why was her own head and heart so confusing? She was supposed to be backing away emotionally from this man.

But she kept her hand firmly on his arm.

Chapter Ten

At 6:30 p.m., Chase pulled up in front of the address Owen had given him, the man having no idea this was his ex's place. A small one-story white house with a red door and black trim. The backyard was fenced, and he could hear happy barks from that direction.

It was just the three of them in Chase's truck; Hannah's mom was watching Danny for the night, and they wouldn't pick him up until tomorrow morning. In the rearview mirror, Chase glanced at Owen sitting in the back seat. For the past fifteen minutes, Owen had been googling border collies and reading aloud interesting details he'd learned. *Did you know border collies are among the most intelligent breeds? Says here border collies were originally bred to herd sheep—I could definitely use a little help there. Even-tempered and eager to please. Gosh, they're good looking dogs,* he'd added, eyes on his phone. Chase could hear a subdued excitement in Owen's voice, as though he wasn't willing to let himself get too excited before he even met the dogs.

Now he could pick apart nuances in the man's voice? Chase wouldn't have thought they'd spent enough time together for that. Then again, he did pay close attention to Owen. This man who was his father.

A stranger just days ago, Chase could have passed him on the street when he'd first arrived and had no idea he was his father, his flesh and blood, the embodiment of a lifetime of Chase's questions and thoughts. Of course, Chase's face would have given *him* away. But suddenly, a confirmation—*yes, I am your father.* A talk—*this is what happened all those years ago.* A handful of hours spent together over the past few days—in which neither brought up anything personal. All culminating in an uncomfortable awareness that Chase was supposed to *feel* something.

Maybe he was supposed to work on feeling something.

Like with Hannah but the opposite. He was supposed to *not* be unable to stop thinking about her. Not be constantly replaying their night together. Not be wondering what was to come. If helping her regain her trust would even lead her to *him*.

In due time, he half-heartedly told himself, reminded of his mother's favorite catchphrase when he was impatient about something.

They all got out of the pickup just as the front door opened and a woman stepped onto the small porch. She had shoulder-length red hair, just like in the photo Owen had stopped on, and wore a pale pink sweater and jeans with cowboy boots.

"Uh-oh," Owen said under his breath. "I didn't—" He stood frozen by the back door of the SUV.

"Owen? Is that you?" the woman asked. She came down from the porch, looking at Owen and then at Chase and Hannah. "I'm Tina Wexler. Are you here to see the dogs?" She looked confused.

"I am, but Hannah texted for me," Owen said. "I didn't realize the ad was yours," he added in a rush.

"Do you two know each other?" Chase asked, hoping his disingenuousness would end up being a *good thing*.

Tina looked at Owen, who was clearly uncomfortable. "We did," she said. "But never mind that. I have two beautiful, sweet border collies who need good homes, and I know you'd provide a great one," she added to Owen.

Phew. Off to a good start on Tina's side of things, anyway.

Chase looked at Hannah, whose eyes slightly widened. Then he glanced at Owen. There was something a bit "deer caught in headlights" about him, as if at any moment he might bolt.

Don't mess this up, Owen, he silently told the man. *Just see where it goes. Don't rush off.*

"They're back here," Tina said, leading the way to the gate to the backyard. She had the gate open and held it for them to pass before Owen could even blink.

Perfect, Chase thought.

The moment they stepped into the yard and saw the dogs, furry black-and-white with floppy black ears, Owen put his hand to his heart. "They're both exactly like the border collie I wanted to adopt when I was a kid," he said, dropping on one knee to give both a good petting. The dogs leaned against him, one of them licking his neck, both wagging their tails.

Tina laughed. "Well, I was going to give you a couple treats so you could make fast friends with them, but looks like that happened automatically."

Owen kept his gaze on the dogs. "You're both good boys, aren't you," he said, continuing to pet them and letting them give him all the doggie kisses they wanted. He grabbed a ball on the ground and stood and threw it, both border collies running to chase it, their ears flopping.

One brought it back, the other staring at him expectantly as if to say: *My turn?*

Owen threw it again, the other dog fetching it this time. "Shep," Owen said with a nod, pointing to the one with the red collar. "And you're Arlo," he added to the one with the blue collar.

Hannah grinned. "Named already. I think the man is sold—and on both!"

"If that's all right with you," Owen said to Tina.

The woman was beaming. "I've been to the ranch, of course, so no home visit is required. And I can personally vouch for your character as a pet owner. I've seen how you treat the livestock at the ranch. And I can pretty much count on them—Shep and Arlo—being welcome not only in the house, but having very comfortable dog beds. Probably memory foam."

Owen's entire body relaxed, and Chase realized what had done it were the words *I can personally vouch for your character.*

His heart went out to Owen at how meaningful that clearly was.

"You'd just need to fill out a proper application," Tina added, "and I'll run it over first thing to the shelter and speak to the director. I can't imagine anything interfering."

"So I might even be able to pick them up tomorrow?" Owen asked her.

"I'll call you in the morning and let you know that everything is settled and what time works. Maybe I can even drop them off at the ranch with the shelter's adoption kit—a couple of cans of their food, favorite treats, toys."

Owen was all smiles. "That would be great." His gaze lingered on Tina's face, and for a moment neither of them said anything.

Romance resparking, Chase thought.

"Why don't we go sit down on the patio and you can fill out the paperwork," Tina said, gesturing at the table and chairs near the back door of the house.

"We'll stay and play with the dogs," Hannah said.

As the pair walked toward the patio, Hannah grabbed Chase's hand and gave it a squeeze.

"Success!" she whispered. "Not just for Owen and Tina—but for both dogs too!"

He grinned. "I was worried on the way here how things would go when they saw first saw each other, but it turned out the best possible scenario."

Hannah's phone pinged, and she pulled it out of her pocket. She gasped. "It's from Jasmine. She says she might be interested in taking me up on my offers about the ranch and the catering, and maybe we can meet for coffee tomorrow." Now it was Hannah putting her hand to her heart.

He wanted to pull her into a hug and hold her tight, but thankfully Arlo dropped the ball at her feet and wagged his tail, his adorable head tilting. After last night, an embrace would be more than just a friendly hug. Every moment of feeling her against his body would come raging back. He both wanted to remember all the details and stop thinking about them, since it was torturous that there would not be a repeat. "I'm glad for you. Lots of good news tonight."

She beamed and read the text again, then put her phone away and knelt down in front of Arlo. "How can I resist this face?" she asked the pooch before petting him and Shep. Then she stood and threw the ball, both dogs running for it.

She turned to him with such a beautiful smile that Chase felt like everything would work out and be okay.

Including with them.

But then he realized he had no idea what exactly that meant. Chase lived in Bear Ridge—five hours away. Even thinking about an extended stay in Winston seemed like he'd be making a major commitment to Owen as his father, to building a relationship, and he didn't feel ready to do that. The plan had been only to get to know Owen, see what kind of person he was.

But Hannah and Danny were here in Winston too.

Shep dropped another ball in front of him, pulling Chase out of his thoughts. But just what *was* he going to do?

At just before nine the next morning, Hannah was on her way to the McCord Ranch to meet Jasmine. She'd called Owen last night to ask about hosting the wedding on the property, and as expected he didn't hesitate in saying yes. *I can't begin to make up for what Kent stole from Jasmine and her fiancé, but I can offer a beautiful spot for the wedding.* The weather had cooperated this morning too—bright sunshine, high fifties, perfect to show off the beauty of the landscape with the mountains in the distance.

As she approached the drive, she took a quick swig of the macadamia nut blend coffee Chase had not only made but poured into her travel mug—fixing it just the way she liked it too. He'd offered to pick up Danny from her parents' for her so she could have the time before leaving for Jasmine's to gear up for it. Mentally prepare. Always thoughtful, that Chase. She was definitely nervous about the meeting this morning, not sure how it would go. If Jasmine was saying okay to the offer but not to friendship. In any case, the meeting was a truce that Hannah would gladly take.

A yawn escaped her, and she took another swig of coffee. Even though Danny had spent the night at her parents' house, Hannah had woken up the usual times that he always did, then found it difficult to get back to sleep. At just after 2:00 a.m., she tried all her tricks, from white noise on her phone to meditative breathing. She'd probably been too excited to sleep. There was Owen reconnecting with his old love. There was Jasmine actually agreeing to talk about Hannah's offer. And there was the man down the hall. A big part of her had wanted to walk right into his room, slip into bed with him and ignore the warnings that had gripped her the morning after. Instead, she'd closed her eyes and let herself remember their night together and then drifting off to sleep, pleasant memories of him spooned against her, how safe she'd felt. How not alone.

But her eyes had popped open a few seconds later as she'd recalled how she'd thought *I love you* in the middle of it all.

Could she have fallen in love despite all the

barriers she'd put up between them? Thick walls. Emotionally running away. Chalking up her emotional response to him to his kindness and generosity and babysitting skills. *You* appreciate him, she'd told herself. *You don't* love him-love him. That was much less scary and she'd forced her thoughts off Chase.

When Hannah pulled into the parking area by the barn, she saw Owen and his part-time ranch hand moving the sheep into a farther pasture. Owen gave her a wave and then came over.

"I heard from Tina this morning," he said, all smiles. "Shep and Arlo have found their forever home. She's bringing them over at eleven."

Hannah grinned. "I'm so happy! They're going to love it here."

"I'm, uh, not sure if you knew, but Tina and I were actually pretty serious when we were dating," he said, tipping up his hat a bit. "I ended things because I didn't want her dragged into the mud with me. Know what she said to that? That she'd stand by me. That crushed me. That she'd be willing to take whatever was flung at her. But it made me even more determined to stay far away from her."

"Sounds like you really cared about her."

He looked off into the distance. "I did."

"Well, today just might be the day for fresh starts. Jasmine's due over any minute."

He brightened. "Chase has sure done a lot of good in a short time for both of us. I wish he lived closer. Once he goes back home, it'll be harder to build the relationship. And it's not like I can try to rush that while he *is* here."

Hannah nodded, trying to hold back her frown. She didn't want to think about Chase leaving. Another week, maybe two was all they had. Staying was no good either because then she'd just fall harder and deeper in love with him. Leaving was no good because *out of sight, out of mind* wouldn't work with a guy like Chase Dawson. She couldn't imagine a day would go by that she wouldn't think of him.

Jasmine's small black car came up the drive. Owen gave a wave. "I'll leave all the arrangements for the wedding to you, Hannah. I don't want to overwhelm her with my presence." He gave her hand a squeeze and then rejoined his employee in the far pasture.

Jasmine got out of her car, shielding her eyes from the bright sunshine as she looked around. "Such a pretty place," she called as she walked over to Hannah. "Even with it scaled back so dramatically, you can't steal nature's beauty."

"Kent did some damage there too," Hannah said. "He forged documents and secretly sold off quite a bit of land on the far edges. If you look closely in one spot, you can make out the weather vanes on the top of the barns that went up."

Jasmine looked like she wanted to spit. "Well, in six weeks, the trees will be all be in full bloom and this place will be even more beautiful."

That was true. "Let's walk out to where I'm thinking we'll set up the tent. It's a breathtaking spot."

As they started off, Hannah wondered if the strain would ever let up between them. Jasmine kept the conversation neutral. How they'd have light till almost 9:00 p.m. in June for the wedding, that she was still deciding between two songs for the dance with her father. They walked a half mile down to open land, wood fencing at the edges, the mountains majestic as the backdrop. Hannah pointed at the place where she envisioned the tent going and the white lights they'd string through the trees. Hannah had called the caterer she used to work for about borrowing tables and chairs and flatware and glasses in exchange for working any events, and her old boss had said that wasn't necessary and she could easily spare what was needed. The muscles in Hannah's shoulders had immediately unbunched. Flowers would be an expense, but with this kind of setting, centerpieces for the tables wouldn't be necessary.

Jasmine looked all around, then took out her

phone and wrote down some notes. "You're probably surprised I changed my mind about this place after what I said yesterday."

Total understatement. "I was hopeful." Also an understatement.

"What you said as I walked away—that stuck with me and I talked to Michael about it. That it's not the same ranch. It's rebuilt from the ashes of what that lying scumbucket did. I guess it's like a fresh start."

Hannah nodded. "Those two words have been coming up a lot these past days."

"You didn't know about Kent, did you," Jasmine said, looking right at her. Not a question.

Hannah shook her head, unable to speak at the moment. She'd been waiting for this for nine months, out of hope most of that time that she'd ever get her friend back. *If* she could get her friend back. Maybe they'd never have the same friendship they'd once shared, but it could be a 2.0 like the ranch was going through. Part of that fresh start.

Jasmine pocketed her phone and then pulled Hannah into a hug, tears in her eyes as she stepped back. Hannah wiped under her eyes too. "I'm so sorry. Really sorry. I was so angry I didn't want to believe you, I guess."

"I can understand," Hannah said. "I almost take

it as a compliment, like you didn't believe I could possibly be so dumb."

Jasmine laughed and so did Hannah. "That's exactly right, actually. But I should have known better. And because of my anger and resentment, I wasn't there for you when you needed me. I wasn't there when you were blindsided by that bastard or for the pregnancy or Danny's birth or the last few months. I'm surprised you even still want to be my friend."

Oh, Jasmine. "We can be there for each other now," Hannah said—hearing the hope infused in her voice.

Jasmine squeezed her hand. "We can be." She glanced at her watch. "I'd better get going. Grooming client at eleven, and it's a ways out from here."

They walked back to the parking area by the barn, Hannah getting some basic info on the date of the wedding—the first Saturday in June; number of people—twenty-four, immediate family and a few friends, which was very manageable; and timing for the ceremony—a 5:00 p.m. start.

As they arrived back at Jasmine's car, she said, "I'll text you about getting together to talk about the food. I know it'll be exceptional now that you're the chef."

Hannah felt herself beam. When Jasmine's car

disappeared down the drive back to the gates, Hannah pulled out her phone and texted Chase.

Jasmine is having her wedding at the ranch! And things are going to be okay between us.

She knew he'd probably arrived at the ranch already to do some work in the office, with Danny as his napping assistant, given the hour, and she hoped he wouldn't mind a small interruption.

He texted back almost immediately—as he always did. A thumbs-up and a smiley face emoji wearing a cowboy hat. Today just keeps getting better. I thought Danny wrapping his little fist around my pinky a little while ago was big.

Hannah felt her heart swell and pulsate. *I love you*, she thought—for the second time in two days—and quickly put her phone in her pocket so she wouldn't text it—or even a big red heart.

Not I *appreciate* you.

Love.

Chapter Eleven

Just twenty minutes ago, Chase had left Hannah and Danny at the ranch—and he already missed them. He'd been in the office, going over the offerings for the cattle auction that he and Owen were now on their way to, when Hannah had come in to take over Danny's care.

She'd been so animated and happy. Over the new beginning she had with her lifelong friend. At seeing her baby boy and cuddling him close, twirling around with him. At having played with Owen's new dogs, Shep and Arlo, who according to Hannah had immediately taken to the ranch, loving the big fenced pasture across from the house, where Tina had set up acclimation shop. Tina was a novice dog trainer and would come work with Arlo and Shep three times a week in exchange for developing her skills. When Hannah relayed that to Chase, they'd both burst into grins. Operation Matchmaking: success. Until he and Owen got back from the auction, Hannah would stay at the ranch with Danny, keeping an eye on the dogs in the pasture. So far, Arlo and Shep had been gentle around Danny, but they would keep the baby separated until the pooches were more settled in their new home.

"Wild, isn't it?" Owen said now as he turned onto the drive for the ranch where the auction was being held. "Seems like overnight, my entire life has changed."

Chase glanced at him. There was a new lightness in Owen's voice—and in his expression. "It really has."

"You—in my life," Owen added. "That would be enough, trust me. And now I have two dogs, border collies I've wanted since I was a kid. And then there's Tina. We, uh, we used to date. And now it looks like we might pick up where we left off. Not to mention I'm on my way to an auction for two additions to the herd that should make a big difference." He shook his head, wonder lighting his face. "I don't know what the heck I did to deserve all this, but man, it feels good."

Chase smiled. "I hear Tina's going to train Shep and Arlo in the ranch boundaries so they can be trusted off leash."

"Yup. I wouldn't know the first thing about that, so I really appreciate her help. They seem well trained in the basics, thanks to her fostering them for the past three weeks. She said they were an elderly owner surrender and were mostly house pets, but she thinks they'll love herding—what they were bred for."

"I saw them scampering around the pasture when we were heading out," Chase said. "They're really good-looking dogs." He pulled out his phone, going to a photo of the two Black Angus cows he had his eye on for the auction. "These gals aren't as pretty as Arlo and Shep, but they'll definitely make a nice addition."

"This will be my first auction since everything came to light," Owen said, his expression hardening a bit. "I tried to attend one way back but a few ranchers ran me off, yelling at how I probably had their hard-earned money in a foreign bank. But between you and the chief giving that presentation and the fact that the ranch clearly doesn't have a dime in profits, I don't think I'll get chased away."

Chase frowned at the picture that formed in

his mind of Owen being run off. How awful that must have been—and how lonely. Betrayed and heartbroken by his son. Shunned by his former community of ranchers.

Owen moved the conversation to how high they'd bid on the cattle, and then asked a bunch of questions about the ranch that Chase worked for. Thinking of the Dawson Family Guest Ranch was a lot more appealing than imagining Owen being chased by cowboys wielding pitchforks.

"Been foreman there long?" Owen asked.

"Over a year," he said. "One of my cousins-in-law was the forewoman, but she wanted to focus solely on managing the dude ranch aspect, so they needed someone to handle the working ranch itself. I'd been a foreman at another ranch and liked the idea of working with family."

Owen's face tightened. And Chase realized that *they* were family, too, he and Owen, and maybe Owen figured Chase wasn't thinking along those lines. Chase supposed he wasn't, actually.

To get off that subject, he shifted gears. "But when my mother died, I started thinking seriously about buying a ranch of my own, something small. My mom always wanted a small ranch, some cattle, goats and chickens. Before I decided to come to Winston and follow that lead on the slip of paper, I was going to look into that in earnest, name it in her memory."

Owen glanced at him. "Lynnie always used to talk about having a dairy farm someday. She'd worked at a farm and had learned how to milk and make cheese and loved the idea of having her own business. She particularly loved goats."

Chase could recall his mother taking him to visit farms and petting zoos on weekends his entire childhood. The goats' antics would make her laugh like nothing else could. "Yeah, those dreams had to be sat on, though," he said. Hopefully not unkindly. Just truthfully. "She had a child to raise completely on her own at age seventeen." He'd always wondered about something and now seemed as good as any time to ask. "Why didn't your parents help her financially? Zero child support? They were wealthy."

Owen frowned. "I'm embarrassed to say that they wanted to wash their hands of her completely. They did leave her five hundred dollars cash. As my parents and I were leaving with Kent, I purposely left my backpack in her room so that I could run back for it and tell her I was sorry, but I could barely get the words out and I just stood there sobbing and stammering. I found the cash back in its envelope in my backpack when I got home. I guess at that point she didn't want anything of theirs tainting the baby she was left with."

Chase swallowed. He could see his proud mother shoving that envelope of cash in Owen's backpack. Returning that money must have been hard. He could also see Owen sobbing, unable to speak. Chase sucked in a breath.

Owen was quiet for a few moments. "Maybe we could buy a couple of goats at the auction in her honor."

A lump formed in his throat. "That's a nice idea."

They were quiet the rest of the way, the sight of the outbuildings and the signs for the auction giving them something else to focus on. The parking area was full of pickups with livestock trailers. As they headed inside the first barn, several ranchers nodded at them, several more stared and even more whispered. Chase figured they had to get that out of their system, not just the con man son aspect but the twins separated at birth part. And now that Owen would be a fixture in the ranching community again, that would likely soon stop.

They stood in front of the pen with the Black Angus cows they were interested in. A few men and women came over to welcome Owen back, some said they were sorry about what he'd been through but they were glad to hear things were looking up for him. And still others were focused on Chase—marveling at how uncanny the resemblance was between him and his twin, even though they *were* identical.

"I don't know," a tall, stocky blond man said, staring at Owen. He stood with a woman and two teenagers. "You abandoned your own newborn. Took one and left one." He shook his head, disgust contorting his features, then looked at Chase. "I'm surprised you'd even want to know him after what he did."

Chase glared at the man. This was the last thing Owen needed. He remembered Owen telling him yesterday about a similar call he'd gotten that had almost derailed Owen's day. "We're here for an auction, not commentary on our personal lives."

The man lifted his chin. "Will someone explain to me how anyone does that?" He threw up his hands and looked around for support.

"Enough," the woman with him harshly whispered to him.

So many pairs of eyes were on Owen. All the light and happiness that had been in Owen's expression just minutes ago, throughout the ride here, were gone. Now, a hard frown pulled at his face.

"Leave him alone," another man nearby said. "He was a teenager. His parents made him do it."

The blond man snorted. "Don't give me that

as an excuse. *I* enlisted in the army when I was a teenager."

Chase shook his head. "Ignore him," he said to Owen.

"I need to get out of here," Owen said to Chase, his voice breaking. He hurried for the exit.

Chase tried to catch up with Owen, weaving his way through the crowd. He found him just outside, hands on his hips, slightly bent over as if catching his breath.

"You okay?" Chase asked, a hand on his shoulder.

Owen didn't respond. He remained slightly bent and then started almost gasping for breath.

Oh no, oh no, oh no. Was he having a heart attack?

Chase pulled out his phone and pressed in 911, frantically relaying the address and begging them to hurry.

A small crowd started forming. "There's a first-aid station staffed by a nurse set up just over there," a woman rushed to say. "I'll go for help!"

Owen was still gasping, and now he was touching his chest.

In seconds, the nurse had rushed over with a wheelchair and had Owen settled. "The ambulance will take him to the clinic for assessment and go from there." She turned to Owen, whose face was both pale and ashen. "You hang on, sir. Help is on the way."

As the nurse checked Owen's pulse, Chase could hear the ambulance coming, his own heart pounding. *Yes, you hang on, dammit. Hang on.*

Let him be okay, he sent silently upward. *Please.*

In minutes Owen was on a gurney, the EMTs loading it into the back of the ambulance. Chase looked anxiously past them at Owen laying so still, an oxygen mask covering most of his face.

"Are you family?" the female EMT asked Chase.

He froze. He opened his mouth to say something but nothing came out. Seconds ticked by.

Owen didn't have seconds.

The EMTs were both staring at him. "Are you or not?" the male one said.

Chase sucked in a breath. "I'm his son."

"Well, come on, then," the woman said, gesturing at him to climb into the back of the ambulance.

Chase sat on a built-in seat along the side, his panic giving way to a strange numbness. Part of him wanted to yell out, *I don't belong here. I don't know this man. Family? I just met him a couple days ago*, and then jump out of the ambulance.

Hold it together for Owen's sake, he ordered himself.

But it was a taller order than he expected.

* * *

Hannah had been pacing in the Winston Urgent Care waiting room since she arrived twenty minutes ago. She'd rushed over from the ranch the moment she got Chase's call. She held Danny against her, which helped keep her somewhat calm and centered. According to a nurse who'd given them an update a little while ago, Owen was still being assessed by a doctor and having an EKG.

"If I get my hands on that despicable human being who had to stick his nose in Owen's personal business and get him all upset," Hannah muttered. "How dare he?"

Chase stopped his own pacing and dropped down onto a chair. "I know. If only people would keep their damned opinions to themselves." He stood up again and moved over to one of the windows. "Everything was going so well up to that point. We were really talking, too. Not just about the ranch."

"Owen will be okay," she told him. "He will be because he has to be. His grandbaby here expects to see him at his Little League games and high school graduation."

Chase's gaze shifted to Danny's face, and Hannah could see his demeanor change a bit, his anxiety ebbing. "Can I hold him for little while?"

"Of course," she said, transferring the baby into Chase's arms.

He sat down, rocking Danny, which seemed to be helping Chase as well.

The bell jangled over the front door and Tina rushed in. "Is Owen okay?" she asked, her tone frantic. Hannah had texted Tina, knowing she'd want to be here.

"They're running tests," Hannah said. "No updates yet."

Now Tina was pacing too. "We just got…reacquainted," Tina said, her eyes misty. "He has to be okay. Shep and Arlo already adore him."

Hannah sat beside her and squeezed Tina's hand just as the door to the exam rooms opened and the nurse returned.

"Owen is going to be just fine," the woman said. "He didn't have a heart attack. It was a panic attack. The symptoms can be frighteningly similar."

Hannah, Chase and Tina all seemed to expel breaths of relief at once.

"Can we see him?" Hannah asked.

"One at a time, please," the nurse said. "He's okay but shaken." She let them know he'd be discharged in about an hour, and that someone should drive Owen home and stay with him for a few hours.

"Tina, why you don't go see him first," Hannah said. "I know you have to get back to your office. We'll take Owen home when he's discharged and stay with him."

Tina stood. "And you'll keep me updated later?"

"Of course," Chase said.

Tina hurried through the door to see Owen.

Hannah leaned back in her chair, resting her head against the wall. "Thank God."

"Hear that, Danny?" Chase said to the baby. "Granddaddy is A-OK."

Tina was back in the waiting room in just a few minutes. "I let him know the three of you are here and that Arlo and Shep were in good hands in the fenced pasture with his ranch hand keeping an eye. He nodded and then said, 'Tell Chase thank you for me,' and a second later was fast asleep."

"We'll let him rest and then take him home," Hannah said.

After saying goodbye to Tina, Chase was up and pacing again, but this time, Danny didn't seem to be calming him down.

"You okay?" Hannah asked. "It was a big scare."

She wasn't sure if he heard her. He didn't respond. His attention was focused out the window, where there were just budding trees as a view.

"I don't know what I am," he finally said, his gaze still out the window.

What are you thinking? she wondered. *You can talk to me.* She wanted to get up and go over to him, put a comforting arm around him, but he suddenly seemed unapproachable and she wasn't sure why.

He stayed quiet, holding Danny, lost in his thoughts.

Just don't shut me out.

Chapter Twelve

Despite three adults, one baby and two dogs, the ranch house was quiet, too quiet for Chase. He needed noise, even some screeching from Danny, definitely some barking, to drown out his thoughts. But Danny was asleep in the nursery that Owen had set up for him in a spare room back when Hannah was pregnant, the dogs were curled up in the plush round beds Tina had brought from her house, Owen was resting in his bedroom and Hannah was baking a birthday cake for a client, which she'd deliver in the morning.

Chase had been sitting in an armchair by the window, once again staring out, now at the night sky. It was just after seven thirty and felt like three in the morning.

He kept thinking about what that jerk had said at the auction. The way he'd felt when he didn't know what was happening with Owen just outside the barn. Panic of his own. And then a casual, everyday comment from the EMT who was loading the gurney holding Owen.

Are you family?

He couldn't stop thinking of how he'd frozen, unable to answer a yes or no question.

I'm his son, he'd finally said.

But those words had felt forced despite being true. When would he feel a bond? Maybe he wouldn't? Maybe twenty-eight years was just too long.

Unsettled, he went into the kitchen to get a beer—but mostly to see Hannah. There were times he looked at her and his thoughts emptied out of his head, replaced by how pretty she was. He could use a big dose of that now.

She paused from stirring a delicious smelling batter. Was there the faint aroma of coconut? "Owen has a much better oven than I do. We were surprised Kent didn't sell it and replace it with one like the twenty-year-old electric kind in my apartment."

"Did you consider living here?" he asked, keeping his voice low. Owen's bedroom was on the first floor, and even though it was clear on the other side of the house, he didn't want to disturb Owen from his rest or be overheard talking about him. "I'm sure Owen asked a few times if you'd move in with Danny."

"He did," Hannah said, also in a low voice. "But like I said that first day we met, it's important to me to pay my own way, have my own home, even if it's a shabby rental. Even if I love the ranch."

Chase nodded. "He's told me twice now that I'm always welcome here." He uncapped the beer and dropped down at the kitchen table.

"You look kind of pained," she said, staring at him. "You okay?"

He told her about the awkward moment with the EMT. His hesitation at answering what should have been a simple yes or no question. But of course it wasn't a simple question.

Are we family if we just met days ago? Are you my father if I didn't know you for almost all my twenty-eight years?

He must have actually said that aloud because Hannah was nodding.

"You were never able to refer to your father your entire life," she said. "The words 'my dad, my father' have never come out of your mouth because there *was* no father, not in name, not in person. Of course you hesitated in answering the EMT, Chase."

That she understood had his shoulder muscles relaxing. "And you want to know where my mind went? If Owen hadn't had the oxygen mask on, would he have piped up with 'He's my son'? I am his son, but…"

"But you're not ready to be claimed. By him or anyone. Actually I take that back. You've let Danny claim you."

Chase realized he was staring at her. She was absolutely right. How was she so right when he hadn't quite thought about it that way himself. He wasn't ready to be claimed.

By Owen…or by Hannah. Here he thought she was the one who needed help regaining her trust in people. But she was out of the starting gate— she'd actually begun there the moment she accepted that he wasn't Kent. And Chase was far behind, not moving.

"Danny makes it so damned easy," he said. "Why is that?"

"Sweet little innocent baby. Even if he demands everything from you—your full attention, your hands, your sleep, your time, your day, your evening. When you do all that a baby requires, you know how capable you are of love and commitment. The baby actually does all the therapy for you. We should pay them for keeping us whole."

Chase laughed but sobered up instantly. She was right again. "But why do I feel a bond with Danny as my *nephew*? That family connection I can't seem to feel with Owen—I feel it with Danny."

She stopped stirring and clanked the wooden spoon on the edge of the bowl. "Because there's no…hard stuff between you two. He might be the son of the twin you never knew about, but he represents the present and future and new beginnings. The word *nephew* is easy. The word *father* is complicated"

"Because DNA alone doesn't make a father. I'd know that even if my mother didn't drill that into me."

"I completely agree," she said. "Being there. Being present. Commitment. Time. Love. Responsibility. That's what makes a father. And a mother."

He nodded. "I'm not sure why any of this heavy conversation made me feel better, but it did. So thank you."

She poured the batter into a cake pan and then slid it in the oven, turning on the timer. "I think it's about understanding," she said, coming to sit down at the table with him. "Not everyone will agree with how you feel or see things as you do right now. Like the guy at the auction who got Owen so upset. He can't see the situation, which he knows nothing about, from other angles or he's unwilling to. That's not someone you want to talk to when you're feeling unsure of your own head."

"Then I'm lucky he's not here and you are."

She smiled and covered his hand with hers, and then he did the same.

And before he knew it, his arms were around her and his lips were on hers, and she was kissing him back. Somehow they ended up against the counter. He could feel every inch of her body against his.

"I'm not so sure this is what you need tonight," Hannah said, pulling away. "This right here—it's about deflecting."

"Or very real attraction."

"Good old-fashioned lust. And then what?" she asked, turning to face him. "You don't know how you feel about a lot going on in your life, Chase Dawson. And you don't have to. I can't be one of those things, though. For my own peace of mind."

He inwardly sighed. She kept being right tonight. "Understood," he said.

"Do you want to be on Danny duty tonight or do you need some time to yourself?" she asked.

"I've got tonight," he said. "I don't think I'll be getting much sleep anyway."

She gave his hand one last squeeze in understanding, then turned to the sink and started scrubbing the bowl and spoon.

This thing between us isn't just about lust, he wanted to tell her. But maybe it had to be.

As expected, Chase didn't fall asleep easily. So when he heard Danny cry out at just after 1:00 a.m., he was glad to have something to do other than lay in bed in Owen McCord's house and stare at the ceiling.

He quickly shoved off the blanket and stood since the bed, the room, the *house* felt so strange. There were five bedrooms—the master on the first floor, the nursery, two guest bedrooms and Kent's childhood room, which Chase had passed and saw was still a teenager's room. Trophies on display shelves. A Winston High School pennant for a state championship. Posters of bands from ten to fifteen years ago. Maybe Kent had gotten his own place when he graduated and Owen had just kept his room as it was when he left. When Kent would stay over, *if* he stayed over, maybe he liked the nostalgia. Chase didn't really care and certainly didn't want to know.

He didn't want to know too much about Kent.

His identical twin. Out there somewhere, likely conning more unsuspecting people with good, trusting hearts.

He went down the dimly lit hall to the nursery, surprised to see Owen coming up the stairs with Danny, who was having his bottle. Chase and Owen were in very similar pj's, he noticed. T-shirt and sweats, though Owen wore sheepskin slippers. "I'll take care of Danny if you need to rest," Chase offered.

Owen looked up in surprise. "Appreciate that, but I feel fine now," he said, carrying Danny to the nursery. He sat down in one of the two cushioned rocking chairs by the window, a small round table between them. "I've been down and up the stairs with no problem. And carrying this little guy after lugging hay bales is nothing."

Chase nodded. He knew that for himself.

"Guess you're a light sleeper like I am," Owen said.

Chase nodded. "I told Hannah I'd take the overnight Danny duty."

"Beat you to it," Owen said with a smile, then gazed down at the baby he held, contentedly suckling on the bottle. "I made that crib," he added, gesturing at the sleigh crib against the wall. "And the dresser. When Hannah told me she was pregnant, that I was going to be a grandfather. Honestly, I don't know what I would have done without that amazing news to think about, to look forward to. Every time Hannah would stop over and her belly was another month bigger, I'd feel hopeful instead of like complete cow dung. Took me three months to get both pieces done. I was just in time."

"Very nice craftsmanship," Chase said, eyeing the furniture.

"Well, I always wanted Hannah to know she'd be comfortable here, that Danny would have what he needed. Those two saved my life at a real low point, you know?"

Chase glanced at Owen, whose eyes were on the baby, his jaw tight. "I'm glad for all three of you. I think you all saved each other."

Owen nodded, then set the empty bottle down and shifted Danny vertically against his chest to burp him, a white cloth on his shoulder.

Danny let out one heck of a burp, and both Owen and Chase laughed.

"There's another cattle auction tomorrow," Chase said. "Next town over. Feel up to it?"

"Absolutely." Owen continued to hold the baby against him, giving his back gentle pats and rubs. "I, uh, won't be caught off guard this time."

"I want you to know that what that guy said— about being surprised I want to know you after finding out what caused the separation… I don't feel that way. I don't hold that against you. If you were older and pulled that on my mother yourself, that would be a different story. But it wasn't your fault."

Owen was quiet for a moment, his head down, and then he looked over at Chase. "That means a lot to me."

"Do you keep Kent's room like it was back in high school because it reminds you of better times?" Chase asked. So much for not caring. For not wanting to know. But he must have been curious from the moment he peeked in the room as he passed it earlier; the question had come out of his mouth without him even thinking about it.

"To be honest, times weren't great then either," Owen said, "but I had no idea how bad things would get, how he'd change. In high school he'd excelled at sports—track and cross-country, baseball—but he'd boast and strut and call out those he didn't think were any good. He got into a lot of fights. He'd be suspended from games and eventually the team. He barely graduated, but he was looking forward to starting a career that would make him good money."

"What type of work was he drawn to?" Chase asked.

"Sales. He had the personality for it. Charming.

Could talk anyone into anything. Of course his looks helped too. He worked in the sales department for a ranch equipment manufacturer and did well since he knew the business, and the McCord name meant something in this county. Being in sales took care of his rough edges and boy, was he smooth. He bought a condo in town just a few months after graduating."

As usual when Chase heard Kent's name or learned something about him, a vague faceless, formless ghost came to mind. This was despite seeing photos of him—one even blown up to 24" x 36" for the presentation at the coffee shop. But this person, his identical twin brother, never felt real.

"I guess I kept his room the same," Owen continued "because he never said anything about packing up the school stuff so I just left it. He stayed over plenty during the past ten years, particularly when he'd pissed off someone's boyfriend or husband. I guess the room reminded him of safer times." Owen shrugged. "But I don't really know. I don't feel like I ever really knew him. That's a terrible feeling."

"Sorry," Chase said, an ache pulsating in his chest.

"Oh, it was much worse when it came to you," Owen added, shifting Danny in his arms so he was semihorizontal again and giving the baby a gentle rock. "I didn't know you at all. Not a thing. That was worse."

Chase swallowed, the ache turning into a lump. Maybe that was why Kent seemed like a ghost. Chase had some information on him, but he'd never met him, never laid eyes on him, and he wasn't sure he ever would.

And if Kent came back to town? Full of apologies and a suitcase of cash to hand out to those he'd wronged, hoping for redemption and to connect with his father and meet his baby son? A second chance with Hannah?

Chills ran up his spine.

No. If Kent came back, it would be very brief, a middle of the night stop for ten minutes on his way somewhere else to maybe say he was sorry to his father, to Hannah, but that he was too far gone, and then he'd disappear again. He very likely would *not* ask to see his baby son. His time in Winston would be so quick he wouldn't even learn that he had an identical twin. That he had a birth mother.

How Chase knew all this, he had no idea. It was just his gut instinct.

"But things are different now, aren't they," Owen said—a statement, not a question. "I feel I *do* know you now. After such a short time."

The middle of the night probably wasn't the

best time to have a talk like this. And Chase didn't feel up to it. He certainly wouldn't talk to Owen about the awkward conversation with the EMT. But hopefully, Owen hadn't even caught that at the time. Given what he'd been going through, Chase doubted he had.

Danny fussed just then. Saved by a fifteen-pound baby.

"There, there," Owen cooed to Danny, standing up and gently swaying him until his eyes fluttered closed. "Let's get you back to sleep, little guy."

Chase stood too. "Well, see you tomorrow. Night, Danny."

He booked out of there and back to his room, which suddenly seemed a lot more comforting than it had twenty minutes ago. He closed the door and slid back into bed, staring out at the inky dark night through the gap in the curtains.

He wished Hannah were here. Lying beside him so he could tell her all about the conversation he'd had with Owen, get her take on it.

Now he was starting to need her. And who was he going to talk to about *that* expected twist?

Chapter Thirteen

Hannah thought she'd gotten up early with Danny at just after 5:20 a.m., but Chase had already made coffee and left a note that he was moving the cattle out to the far pasture and then would be repairing some fencing. She was meeting Jasmine at 8:00 a.m. at the coffee shop to plan the wedding menu, and as she left the house with Danny, she peeked in the barn to see if Chase was there, but he wasn't. She shielded her eyes against the bright April sunshine, hoping to at least get a last glimpse of him, but she didn't see him anywhere.

She got Danny settled in his car seat, then

found herself bringing her fingers to her lips as memories of her kiss with Chase last night floated through her mind again. She'd called a halt to it, knowing Chase needed to deal with his emotions about his father but she wasn't so sure he would anyway. There was a block there still. As she got into her car and started the engine, she wondered if that block would keep him in town longer to work on it or if he'd leave once he thought the ranch had shifted into the right direction.

Fifteen minutes later, she arrived at the coffee shop and wheeled in Danny, whose drooping eyes and yawns told her he'd likely sleep through her meeting with Jasmine. Her friend waved at her and popped up, and they headed to the counter together and stood in the short line.

"Aww, Danny is so precious," Jasmine said, her gaze soft on the already sleeping baby.

Hannah's heart soared. She could still barely believe, after so long, that she had her friend back. She knew rebuilding the friendship would take some time, but that was just fine. "He's a super easy baby. I got lucky there. Champion napper. He does wake up every four hours but with Uncle Chase around, like last night, I've been catching up on sleep."

Jasmine's eyes widened. "Oooh, so Chase handles nighttime feedings?"

"He's making himself a little too indispensable," Hannah said. It was their turn to order. Hannah went for a cappuccino and toasted bagel with cream cheese. Jasmine chose an iced vanilla latte and a mixed berry scone.

"Is there something going on between you two?" Jasmine asked, leading the way to a table.

"There is a lot going on between us," Hannah said, plopping down and taking a sip of her coffee. "Maybe more to do with the circumstances than anything else."

Jasmine took a bite of her scone. "Way I've always seen it is that attraction is attraction and chemistry is chemistry. It's either there or it's not. And if it's there, it's a speeding train."

She thought about that very quick kiss last night—that would have turned into something more very fast. There was no doubt of the attraction and chemistry between her and Chase. "I guess I'm just trying to find reasons why it won't work out. He'll be leaving by the end of the month, maybe even sooner depending on how quickly he can get things straightened out at the ranch for Owen."

"That was before he knew he had other reasons to stay, though," Jasmine said. "Like his relationship with Danny. If he's doing nighttime feedings and changing diapers, he's *invested*, Hannah."

"In his baby nephew, yes. But I'm another story. And so is Owen. Chase seems really conflicted about where to take that relationship. If he even wants one, to be honest." This felt so good, to be talking to Jasmine like old times about their every thought and feeling, their hopes and worries.

"I can understand that. It's impossible to go from zero to sixty just like that."

Hannah nodded. "I can see it, though. The two of them getting close, I mean. They're both such good people. And they have ranching and Danny in common. Plus all that…tough history. They can bring so much to each other's lives."

Jasmine took a bite of her scone. "I guess Chase has to take it day by day."

That was definitely true. A father-son relationship out of absolutely nothing, with the "tough history" Jasmine noted, couldn't be rushed or faked. It had to develop. And that would take time and trust.

"Warms the heart, I tell you!" a familiar voice said, and both Jasmine and Hannah turned. Hannah's mother had come in, her reading glasses on a beaded chain around her neck. "To see you two together again." Bettina patted her heart.

Jasmine smiled. "We're going to plan the wedding menu. I know anything Hannah cooks will be amazing."

"And I'll be her trusty assistant," Bettina said. She bent down to drop a kiss on sleeping Danny's head. "I'm so happy to contribute to your wedding, Jasmine. You've always been like an honorary daughter to me."

"Aww," Jasmine said, her eyes misty. "I love that."

Bettina smiled at them both. "Well, I'd better order. It's my turn to pick up the caffeine boost for the tellers." She gently smoothed Danny's hair, then headed up to the counter.

"Speaking of wedding menus," Hannah said, "I'd love to hear what you have in mind." She took a bite of her bagel.

"I'm not really sure. I read in a wedding magazine that I should avoid anything too messy. So maybe not saucy pasta? What do you think for an outdoor early summer wedding?"

"Hmm, we could do a three course dinner," Hannah suggested. "Oooh, a Panzanella salad? It's a Tuscan dish, sautéed French bread in olive oil with tomatoes and onions and peppers and cuke. And maybe a grilled chicken in a lemon-herb sauce with spring vegetables or an interesting rice. I can also make vegetarian entrée too—like a porcini or squash ravioli. And for dessert, wedding cake, of course. I remember you always said when you got married you would want a five-tier red velvet wedding cake with those adorable bride and groom toppers." With a guest list of twenty-four people, this menu was definitely manageable. A lot of work, but Hannah could do it, thanks to her mom's help. Maybe even Chase's as prep guy. Cake pan greaser.

"I haven't changed a bit," Jasmine said with a grin. "That all sounds perfect! You go with whatever detail choices sound good. I trust you."

Hannah leaned over and pulled her friend into a hug. Those words meant everything to her. And if Jasmine could trust her after holding back for so long, then maybe Hannah could let herself trust Chase not to stomp on her heart.

"Who knows," Jasmine said, sipping her latte. "Maybe they'll be a wedding in *your* immediate future."

"Ha, we couldn't even get through a *kiss* last night. I don't see a wedding."

Jasmine raised an eyebrow. "Well, there *was* a kiss, and where there is one, there will be another!" She smiled. "The amazing thing about life is that you can't rule out anything. Very unexpected things happen every day. Little miracles."

Hannah glanced at Danny, sleeping so peacefully in the noisy coffee shop. He'd certainly been unexpected. A *huge* miracle. Something beautiful that had come out of the ashes of something awful.

So maybe Hannah wouldn't rule anything out.

Over the next few days, Chase tried not to think so much and just…be. He and Owen had gone to the other cattle auction, and two Black Angus cows had joined the small herd along with two goats, one white and brown, one black with a white nose. There's been some whispers and pointing, but no accusations, no personal comments about the story. He and Hannah had gone back to her apartment since Owen was A-OK after that first night. Chase had thought he'd feel more comfortable at her place, but the tight quarters meant being even more aware of her as they squeezed past each other in the kitchen, Chase preparing a bottle for Danny, Hannah cooking for a client. For the past two nights she'd tried out recipes for Jasmine's wedding, and he was both her assistant and her taste-tester. Talking, sharing, laughing, eating.

There had been no more kisses, let alone sex that had managed to both completely rejuvenate him and tie him in knots.

But things did seem to be progressing between Owen and Tina. She'd been at the ranch to train the dogs, and Chase had seen the couple walking hand in hand yesterday, Shep and Arlo happily scampering ahead, tails wagging.

Good for you, Chase had thought. Owen was definitely happier these days.

Now, Chase was in the barn, mucking out the goats' stall, which those imps had turned upside down in no time.

"I can watch those two for hours."

Chase turned to find Owen standing at the edge of the pen, looking through the double window at the small side pasture, where the goats were taking turns jumping onto a log. "Me too. I can see why my mom was so fond of goats." The ranch would raise them to sell down the line, so they weren't exactly pets who'd have names, but every time Chase saw these two, he thought of his mother and how if she were here, they would make her smile.

Owen was about to grab a rake when his phone rang. He listened for a moment, then said, "Yes, this is Owen McCord of Winston, Wyoming. Yes, I have a son named Kent Eli McCord."

Chase froze and turned to Owen, whose expression had tightened. What was this about? Who was on the other end of the phone?

Owen was listening to whatever the person was saying, then let out a gasp, a strangled sob and dropped onto his knees on the hay bordering the pen. He took off his Stetson and held it against his chest, his eyes squeezed shut.

"Owen?" Chase said, his heart starting to pound. "What's going on?"

Owen glanced at him—miserably, then stared straight down, the phone still clutched to his ear. "Yes," he whispered into the phone. "Yes. All right." Then he dropped the phone beside him and buried his face in his hands.

Chase got down on his own knees beside Owen and put a hand on his shoulder. "What is it?" he asked gently.

"There was an accident," Owen said, his voice rough and breaking. "Stretch of freeway near the Las Vegas strip. It was three days ago, but Kent had so many fake IDs that it took local police a while to identify him. They want me to come out and positively ID the body."

Oh God.

"He was going over a hundred miles an hour late at night in drizzly conditions," Owen added, then started sobbing hard, his shoulders shaking.

"I'm so sorry," Chase said, extending his full arm around Owen's shoulders. "I'm so sorry."

Owen gripped a post of the pen and stood up. "I need to get to Vegas. I'll head to the airport and try to get on any soon-to-depart flight." He swiped under his eyes.

"I'll go with you," Chase said, standing too.

Owen held up two hands. "I appreciate that, but I think I need to do this alone." He wiped under his eyes again. "And I might be wrong, but I don't think your only memory of the twin you never got to meet should be seeing him dead in a morgue."

Owen was probably right about that, but Chase couldn't think straight about it one way or the other. "I'd go to be there for you," he said. "It wouldn't be about Kent. It would be about you."

Owen put a hand on his arm. "I'll be all right. I need to do this on my own."

Chase wasn't so sure about that or if it was a good idea. But it seemed settled for Owen, and Chase knew he had to let it go.

Owen turned to him. "You'll tell Hannah?"

Chase nodded. "I'll go do that now."

With that, Owen put his Stetson back on and left the barn, and only then did Chase realize his legs were trembling.

Chapter Fourteen

Chase had stood in the barn for a good ten minutes, barely able to think or process what he'd just heard, all Owen had said, that he was headed to Vegas alone, when he realized he had to get in touch with Hannah. He was about to text her to ask where she was when she rushed into the barn, Danny in his stroller.

His identical twin, who'd he never met, was *really* gone now.

He leaned his head back and sucked in a breath, then turned to Hannah.

"When I was pulling in just now, I saw Owen with a duffel over his shoulder getting into his truck," she said, hurrying over to him. "I called out a 'hi' and 'romantic getaway?' and he looked at me with the saddest expression, Chase. Then he looked down at Danny and wiped at his eyes and got in the truck and peeled out. What happened? What's going on?"

He reached for her hand and then let it go and told her everything that had happened, the call, Owen sinking to his knees and sobbing, that he wanted to go on his own to Las Vegas.

Hannah's face paled and she stared at Chase, then at Danny. "I need to sit down." She reached for the end post of the stall, and he hurried over to where a few folding chairs were leaned against the wall, grabbed two and unfolded them by Danny's stroller.

He helped her down, then sat beside her. "It's a shock."

Hannah nodded, her eyes downcast. "I just think about Danny, you know? How it would be to grow up knowing your father had to flee town, the police starting an investigation into his cons, that he destroyed his grandfather's ranch. Wondering all the time if his father would ever come back, want to know him."

Chase felt his shoulders sink heavily. He nodded.

"I know this is probably naive of me," she said,

"but these past nine months, for Danny's sake, I'd think about potential redemption. Like, Kent could come back and return everyone's money and vow to change and then actually work on being a decent human being."

"Holding out for hope isn't naive," Chase said. "It means you believe in *good*, that you have faith."

"But now there's no redemption path," she said, tears streaming down her face. "Kent's dead. Danny will grow up knowing what his father did and that he died as recklessly as he lived, driving over a hundred miles an hour." She buried her face in her hands and sobs wracked her body. "What do I tell him?" she managed to whisper. "When he's five, when he's ten, when he's fifteen?"

He turned his chair to face hers directly and took both her hands. "You tell him what you believed. That his father might have come back and worked hard to change who he was. But that he didn't get that chance."

Hannah sniffled and brightened a bit. "I could tell him that. And then I give him that sense of hope."

Chase nodded. And then she flew against him, and he wrapped her in his arms. His head against hers. "I'm so sorry, Hannah. I never wanted to think too much about the fact that he was out there somewhere. But…" He trailed off, not even sure what he meant to say.

She pulled away, taking all that necessary warmth with her. "I think I understand, Chase. You discover you have an identical twin in the same breath you learn he's a con man who did a lot of damage. I wouldn't know how to feel about him either if I were you."

"That's exactly it. I don't know how to feel. I can't stop thinking about what-ifs. What if we'd grown up together? Would we have been close? Would he have still had the gambling problem? Would he have conned people? Betrayed his own father? Would he have left you and Danny? His emotional life would have been completely different with a brother—a twin, at that. But who knows? Maybe I'm more like him than I even know."

Hannah shook her head. "What-ifs are dangerous. You and Kent might have the same DNA but you're not the same person. Kent had a great dad and from what you tell me, a great biological mother, and he was who he was. Anyway, if his emotional life were different, we might not even have met. There might be no Danny. We can only go with what we know and what is. But I do remember what he said when I told him I was pregnant. 'I'm going to be a father? Poor kid.' What a thing to say about yourself, to believe about yourself. That's one thing I won't tell Danny."

They were both quiet then. Chase took her hand and led her over to the double window in the pen. "We got those goats a couple days ago. Watch them for ten seconds and they'll make you smile even if you have no smile in you."

The brown-and-white one was jumping on and off the log while the other watched as if he were shaking his head at the tomfoolery.

"Would you look at that—two seconds," he said, tipping up her chin. "And not to make that beautiful smile falter, but I can't stop thinking about Owen going out to Vegas all alone. Taking care of everything without anyone *there*."

"Let's go too," she said. "I'll text my clients that I need to leave town and list some back-up personal chefs and caterers they could contact."

Chase nodded. They absolutely should go. "Owen said he didn't think my only memory of the twin I never met should be of him in a morgue."

Hannah seemed to think about that for a moment. "It won't be the only one. Maybe this is where those what-ifs come in handy and do some good. *Those* can be the memories. That maybe things would have been different." She looked at Danny, fast asleep in his stroller. "And maybe years from now, Danny will like knowing that he was there, to say goodbye. That might bring him some peace."

Chase pulled Hannah into a fierce hug, his eyes misting. She held on to him tight and he never wanted to let go.

"I'm so sorry to interrupt," a female voice said. Chase turned to see Tina waving at him from the doorway of the barn. "But I was supposed to meet Owen for a training session. Can't find that man anywhere."

Chase took a step back. He took Danny's stroller, and he and Hannah walked to meet Tina. He explained what happened and what they were going to do.

"Oh, you two are good people," Tina said, her eyes compassionate. "I don't claim to know Owen McCord so well—we dated only a couple months before he ended things last year and now it's so new, but I have no doubt he needs you there. All three of you."

Hannah gave her a hug.

"And I'll take Shep and Arlo home with me till you're all back," Tina said. "Don't you worry about a thing."

"You're good people yourself," Chase said. "I'm sure Owen will be relieved to hear they're with you."

Within a half hour, they were packed and ready to go. Chase had spent a few minutes trying to figure out which flight Owen might be taking, and when he'd arrive in Las Vegas. A few airlines had flights to Vegas within the hour, but it was doubtful Owen would make any of those. But trying to get to the airport and find Owen would be difficult among the various airlines and gates; it would waste valuable time. Based on how long it took to get the airport and when the next flights left, Chase figured out a reasonable arrival time. He called a private plane company and booked a flight for himself, Hannah and Danny. They should arrive around the same time as Owen, no matter which airline he flew.

He might not know how he felt about Owen McCord. Or Kent. But he knew he had to be there for this tender, taciturn, heartsick man he was coming to know.

And an hour later, when Chase was buckling his seat belt on the small plane and looked to his right, he counted his blessings that Hannah and her baby son were with him.

Hannah dropped down on the queen-size bed in the bed-and-breakfast just outside Las Vegas. She glanced to her left; Danny was napping in the Pack 'N Play the B&B owner had lent them.

She wondered how things were going for Chase and Owen. Before they left for the private airport back in Wyoming, Chase had texted Owen that they were on their way and not turning back no matter what, and that Chase would meet him at the Clark County coroner's office. Owen had texted back right away what time his plane's ETA and then added, Thank God you're coming anyway and brought much-needed reinforcements. I'm shaking like a November leaf.

Chase had held up the phone for her to read the text and then gave her hand a squeeze. For a long moment, they'd just sat like that, his hand on hers, and she had no doubt Chase's heart was as heavy as hers was. For the next while he'd stared out the window, lost in his thoughts, and she let him be. When they'd arrived, they'd decided that Chase would meet Owen and accompany him inside the morgue. Hannah and Danny would head to the B&B that Chase booked, and that was the way they all wanted it. She didn't like the idea of Danny being at the coroner's office or a part of that. It was enough that he was here. That he'd always know he was there with his family. Owen. Danny. Hannah.

And Hannah could say her goodbye, in her own way.

Chase had booked three rooms, but when she'd

arrived, there had been a mix-up and there were only two rooms available. She was more fine with that than she thought she'd be. Sharing a room with Chase, especially under very fraught circumstances, could lead places it would be hard for Hannah to return from. But she didn't want to sleep alone tonight, and she doubted Chase did either. Even if they just shared the bed, held hands like on the plane. Or spooned, the way he had against her the night they'd made love. Oh, how comforting that had been. She'd felt so cocooned.

She must have dozed off because she bolted upright at the sound of gentle knocking on the door, and a glance out the window showed her the sun had set. Danny was still napping in the playpen.

"Hannah? It's me."

Chase. She hurried to the door and opened it. He looked completely spent. She opened her arms and he stepped into them, and they backed into the room, his foot closing the door.

"I saw him," he whispered, his voice cracking. "Kent." He glanced down at the floor for a moment, then at her. "Owen nodded at the coroner, and he pulled the sheet back up, but I saw him, my twin brother." He dropped down on the bed, his eyes downcast. "Owen made the arrangements, and then we were outside again, waiting for an Uber. He didn't say a word on the ride here, and then just stopped at the desk to ask for his room number and the key. I'll let him be for a while, then maybe we'll go see him about ordering in dinner. Even if we eat in silence."

"That sounds like a good plan," she said.

"You okay?" he asked, lifting his head to look at her.

She nodded. "Danny and I were walking through the back garden about an hour ago. There were all these paths and lattices and blooming vines. I said my goodbyes to Kent, to the past, there and I told Danny what you suggested. That I believed his father might have come back at some point to make amends, to meet him and know him because Danny is just too wonderful not to know. But that his father wouldn't get that chance and we were here to say goodbye."

Chase looked at Danny in the playpen. "That's good closure for both of you. Or a start anyway."

She nodded, her gaze on her son. Then she looked back at Chase. "What about you? Are *you* okay?"

He gave a dejected shrug. "I just feel so damned numb. This whole situation—the crazy truth of it and terrible end—is… I don't know what."

"I know exactly what you mean." She got into bed and patted the space beside her. Chase got under the covers with her and stared up at the ceiling. But then he reached for her hand under the blanket and just held it, neither of them saying a word.

Owen had been amenable to ordering in dinner from a bar and grill nearby, and they ate at the table near the sliding glass door to the balcony of his room, the B&B proprietor kindly bringing two extra chairs. Owen and Chase had gotten the New York strip and steak fries, Hannah the linguini carbonara she wasn't sure she'd have much appetite for.

What helped was how a little while ago, Danny had had his own dinner, drinking contentedly from his bottle, none the wiser about anything going on around him. Now, he sat in his stroller, batting at the little stuffed monkey that Owen had picked up in an airport gift shop, always thinking of Danny no matter the circumstances. The baby's big laughter when the monkey ears shook made them all smile, lifting the somber mood. They'd stay the night and all fly back, via private plane again, thanks to Chase, in the morning.

Owen's phone rang. For the second time in the past half hour. And for the second time, Hannah saw him glance at the screen but not pick it up to answer. Hannah was sitting next to Owen and could easily see it was Tina calling again.

Don't shut her out, Hannah thought, trying to telepathically reach Owen. *You need her now. Let her be there for you.*

"I noticed that was Tina's name that popped up on your screen," Hannah said, risking being a buttinsky. "Again," she added as casually as she could.

Owen didn't look up from the steak fry he was forking. "I'm just not in any state of mind to talk."

"Hearing what Shep and Arlo are up to might lift your spirits," Chase said, swiping his own steak fry in ketchup. "I swear those dogs always look like they're smiling."

Owen eyed the phone, which had stopped ringing. He ate his fry but still didn't look up. Then he cut into his steak as if to have something to do. "How'd Danny fare on the plane?"

Hannah glanced at Chase; he too seemed to realize Owen was shutting down the conversation, and he had every right but dammit, Hannah wanted him to call Tina and find comfort in her voice, her compassion. And to hear a funny story about the dogs.

"He was gnawing away on his pacifier when he wasn't napping, so he did pretty well," Hannah said.

"You're a champion baby," Owen said, smiling at his grandson, a forkful of steak in the air.

But his eyes suddenly filled with tears, and he dropped his fork on the plate. "I had some stupid hopes that Kent would come back, make restitution, beg for forgiveness. Look me in the eye and tell me he went temporarily insane because of the stress or whoever was after him about his gambling debt. And that he'd want to be part of this family." Tears streamed down Owen's cheeks. "I look at Danny, and I can't believe what Kent allowed himself to miss out on. And now we'll never have him back."

Hannah almost gasped. That was just what she'd realized earlier. The two of them were the only people on earth who had reason to want that good path for Kent. His father and the mother of his child.

"I told Danny in the garden earlier that I believed his father might have come back, just like you said. Made amends, paid everyone back, a real redemption journey. All so he could be the father Danny deserves. Chase helped me see telling Danny that would instill the same sense of hope and faith I want to have. And I felt better about everything once I told him. Kent won't have the chance for all that. But I think he would have come back. Eventually."

Owen sniffled and wiped under his eyes. "I think so too, Hannah. Eventually."

"And Danny will grow up thinking that too," Chase said. "When he has questions about his father that no one can possibly answer, he can turn to that. And he'll always know he was here now."

Hannah glanced at Chase, realizing that he never had that when he was growing up. No one to ask questions because his mother simply wouldn't say a word about his father, even his identity, his name. He'd known absolutely nothing for twenty-eight years. She could imagine the scenarios he must have run through his head at various ages. At four, his dad was a soldier off fighting for his country in a faraway place. At seven, a swash-buckling spy. At eleven, an astronomist figuring out how to save the planet from a growing black hole. At fifteen, a likely awareness that *something* had happened between his parents, a lack of interest in parenthood from his father, a big fight, *something*, that had led to his mom's refusal to talk about him. She could certainly understand the big void in Chase's heart, the trouble he was having connecting the word father to the flesh and blood man who was suddenly in his life.

There was a time when Hannah thought she'd have only one thing to tell Danny about his absentee father. That he was a lying con man, a betrayer of family, a terrible human being.

Not that she would have said any of that. But

now, she had something kinder to tell him as he grew up.

Owen nodded. "That does make me feel better." He forked a fry. "I feel like you're getting forgotten here, Chase. This is your identical twin we're talking about. It has to weigh on you."

Chase explained about the what-ifs, how they made him feel less disconnected from his own birth story, his own twin. The wondering and speculating. Maybe this, maybe that, if this, then that. Maybe, maybe, maybe. "There's no way to know, of course," he said, "but the not knowing helps. Because then I get to come to some flimsy conclusion that makes me feel better about things."

Owen managed a chuckle, and Chase saw Hannah brighten because of it. "It's how I've gotten through my whole life." He looked at Danny, his expression happier. "Can he spend the night with his grandpop?"

Hannah smiled. "Of course. "We'll bring over what he needs after dinner. Don't expect to get a wink of sleep."

"Eh, sleep wasn't gonna happen anyway," Owen said. "Having Danny stay with me tonight will do wonders for my head."

Just like Chase will for me. And me for him.

"Hear that, Danny?" Owen said. "You'll stay

with your grandpop tonight. I'll tell you a few of those bedtime stories you like about the cow named Big."

A peace settled inside Hannah as she watched Owen smile at Danny. She had no doubt he was grieving deeply, but he was surrounded by family right now. And she'd nudge him toward letting Tina in too. Hannah *was* a buttinsky, but sometimes you had to be. Just like Chase had said he was going to Vegas despite Owen telling him he'd go alone, and then she said she and Danny were coming too. Instead of being alone in some hotel room, Owen was with people who cared about him.

They'd all get through this together.

If Chase would stay in Winston long enough for that to happen.

Chapter Fifteen

As Chase headed outside to the car he'd rented to grab their bags, a little white sports car pulled in with a Just Married sign, and dangling cans all over it. A man in a white tux and white cowboy hat got out of the driver's side and ran to the passenger door and opened it, bowing.

"M'lady," he said with a wide sweep of his arm.

A giggle emerged from the car. A petite woman, her blond hair in two braided coils on either side of her head like Princess Leia, and wearing a poufy white wedding gown, stepped out. The groom scooped her up and kissed her very, very passionately. For a *while*.

When they came up for air, Chase called, "Congrats," since they were like two feet away from him.

"Thanks!" the bride said, her eyes sparkling with happiness and liquor. "We just came from the Strip! We're finally married! Three years of dating, two breakups, two make-upsies, a long engagement and we're finally *one*!" They started kissing again, the bride also still in the groom's arms.

Since his hands were full, the groom kicked the car door shut. "We wanted a little more privacy from all that nonstop activity so we booked our wedding night here in the Fantasy Suite," he said to Chase. "Apparently the bed has a remote control that does all kinds of interesting things." He wiggled his eyebrows and turned to his bride, who giggled some more.

Chase was actually a little curious, but he wasn't about to ask "like what?"

"You married?" the bride asked Chase as the groom began to walk her toward the porch steps.

"Nope," Chase said.

"Aww," she singsonged. "I'll give you my *best* advice. When you find what you need, never let it go. That's the key to life. What you *need*. Forget everything else, all the crap."

"So true, baby," the groom said, and kissed

her all the way up the steps and into the B&B. He heard the proprietor congratulating them and then the couple launching into the same tale. *We just came from the Strip...*

Chase pulled the bags from the trunk of his rental vehicle and then leaned against it, looking up at the starry night, the almost crescent moon.

When you find what you need, never let it go.

He needed Hannah. Hannah needed him.

And then an idea slammed into his head.

Marriage.

We'll be a family. You, Hannah, Danny.

And Owen.

He'd get Hannah out of that cramped apartment. He'd invest money in the McCord Ranch and build it up much faster; Owen would be on his way again and could go back to running the place instead of the slow uphill climb they were currently on. He'd adopt Danny if Hannah was on board with that and give him his family name. He'd give that baby everything he needed. Chase's love, time, devotion.

He'd go to sleep every night with beautiful Hannah beside him, wake up to her every morning.

It was a life plan and good one.

He slung each bag over a shoulder and headed inside, not feeling so numb anymore.

He had *purpose*.

* * *

Hannah had been standing on the balcony of their room when the bride and groom made their appearance. She'd smiled when Chase congratulated them.

But the smile faltered when she'd heard what the bride had said. *When you find what you need, never let it go.*

Hannah needed Chase and never wanted to let him go.

She'd watched the newlyweds kiss their way over to the porch, and then Chase leaned against the truck and stared up at the sky. She wondered what he was thinking.

Then again, he probably wasn't thinking. It had been one hell of a day, very emotional, and stressful. Tonight they'd probably do more of what they had earlier, just lie in bed and hold hands and stare at the ceiling, trying to process their thoughts or not, without having to say a word. They'd just be together, taking comfort in each other.

When Chase came in with their bags, he dropped them by the door. He looked different somehow. Yes, she thought as she studied him. He was…more spirited. When he'd left the room a few minutes ago, he seemed to have the world on those broad shoulders. But now there was determination in his blue eyes. The newlyweds had been funny and maybe they just cheered him up a little.

"So what do you think that remote control does exactly to the fantasy suite bed?" she asked.

He tilted his head as if he had no idea what she was talking about, then he laughed. "Oh yeah—I was wondering that myself. So you heard all that?"

"Yup. I was out on the balcony. 'When you find what you need, never let it go. That's the key to life. What you *need*. Forget everything else, all the crap.' I wonder what 'all the crap' refers to." She chuckled.

"All the not-important stuff, I guess. Lust. Liking the same movies. Enjoying parties."

"Ah. I guess," she said.

"Hannah," he began, but then didn't say anything.

Hmm. He seemed very serious at the moment. She waited for him to talk. But he just looked at her. And kept looking.

Finally, he walked up to her and took both her hands. "*You're* what I need. I think I might be what you need. We've found each other, and we should never let each other go."

She felt her neck stretch out a bit like a turtle as her eyes widened. *This* was unexpected. Chase Dawson was taking advice from a drunk stranger? A happy newlywed, but still. "What do you mean?"

"I mean that we should get married," he said. "Marry me, Hannah Calhoun. I'll adopt Danny. I'll invest in the McCord Ranch and it'll soon be on its way. Danny's legacy will be preserved."

She stared at him and suddenly needed to sit down, the air having whooshed out of her. She backed herself to the bed and dropped down. "And..." she prompted.

"Now I don't know what *you* mean."

"I mean...that's it?" she asked. "That's your reasoning for getting married?"

He nodded, his blue eyes soft and sincere on her. "I think we'd share in a very good life to-gether."

She bit her lip. He was forgetting something. A very *big* something. "I think I just figured out what the bride meant by 'forget all the crap.' Not just lust and common interests. I think she was talking about *love*."

"Love?" he repeated, sitting down in the desk chair across from her.

"Couples start out madly in love, and then it kind of develops into love-love. Not pawing each other three times a day. Companionable silence as you binge watch a show and share popcorn. I think she's discounting being in love. *I* can't."

"Need trumps love, don't you think?" he asked. "Need is everything. You *need* that person. You need that person like air and shelter."

He needed her. But he didn't love her. Wasn't in love with her, certainly.

"Chase, I appreciate you. I really do. How much you care. But for me to get married, after everything I've been through, what I *need* is to be loved by my husband. Madly, truly, deeply. The whole thing."

She waited for him to say, *Of course I love you, Hannah. I love you. I love you* and *need you.*

But he seemed kind of…flummoxed. Unsure of himself.

He'd wanted to give her back her faith and trust in people, and he had. So now she was in love with him.

But it turned out he couldn't give her what she needed, after all.

She felt her heart plummet. "Chase, I think it's incredibly kind that you're motivated by a sense of responsibility for me and Danny and Owen. But that's not a reason to get married."

"Isn't it?" he asked. "Isn't it the best reason? I want to take care of you all. I want us to be together as a family."

So did she. So much. The thought of spending her life with Chase, this beautiful man—inside and out—by her side, her partner in all things, would be a dream come true. *If* he loved her. But she'd told him straight-out that *that* was what she needed, and the words still hadn't come out of his mouth.

He was looking at her hopefully.

She took a breath. He just didn't seem to understand. Which meant they were planes apart. And there would be no celebrating their future tonight.

At breakfast the next morning in the B&B's dining room, Hannah and Chase had been so quiet that even Owen asked if anything was wrong, and he was usually one to stay out of people's business. Hannah tried to perk up and had complimented proprietor June Wendello on the French toast with its powdered sugar and cinnamon and excellent maple syrup. And Chase had made a little small talk about the Hoover Dam with another set of guests, a couple with a teenage son. But when the newlyweds came down the stairs and sat down at the table next to theirs, arm in arm, drinking their orange juice and coffee that way, kissing in between bites of their French toast, dabbing syrup off each other's lips, Hannah said she'd better go change Danny even though she was fibbing about needing to and practically ran from the room, her baby in her arms. No one needed more of their advice or lovey-dovey ways. As she was leaving, she'd been able to hear Chase asking June if he could be of any help clearing the table.

Oh, Chase. Helpful even when he was trying to escape. June had declined his offer and seemed to sense the mood at their table, and sent him and Owen outside to the side patio to enjoy the morning breeze and a fruit salad.

She and Chase been quiet the night before, each taking to the far side of their bed, which had felt a lot smaller than a queen. They didn't even have Danny as a buffer since he was with Owen.

At one point, as they'd been in bed, both facing away from each other, he'd asked, "Maybe you've had some time to think about my proposal?"

As if I've thought of anything else since. "My response would be the same," she'd said around the lump in her throat.

He hadn't said anything to that.

The drive back to the airport and the small plane ride to Wyoming had also been mostly in silence. Owen had looked from Hannah to Chase a few times with question in his eyes, but turned his attention to Danny. Clearly he could tell there was something amiss.

Oh, nothing, Owen, it's just that Chase wants to get married because we need each other. Forget all that crap like love!

When they arrived back in Wyoming, Chase said he'd drop off her and Danny at her apartment and then go straight to the ranch with Owen to do some work in the office. Phew. She needed some space from him and his out-of-the-blue marriage proposal. But as they pulled up in front of her building, Hannah felt her eyes well with tears and hoped no one noticed.

Once, the thought of a marriage proposal from the abstract man she loved would fill her with happiness about the future, the "some day" she'd long dreamed of. Finding her Mr. Right, becoming a unit, a partnership, a pair. Her person, forever. And then the Kent debacle took quick care of those fantasies. She'd gone from thinking Kent would propose, that she was *his* person, *his* Ms. Right, that she was special to him unlike all the women who'd come and gone before her, that they'd marry and have three children, to being a single mother, alone. Daydreams had been knocked out of her, and now her life was about reality. Raising her son on her own, making ends meet, scrimping and saving to pay back her parents what they'd lost to Kent. Some might say she should thank her lucky stars that Chase Dawson was so upstanding, such a believer in responsibility, in taking care of family, that who was she to turn down an offer like his.

But if all the hope went out of her, then what did she really have? What could she teach Danny about life?

As Chase got out to grab her bag, Owen leaned forward from the back seat. "You two in a tiff?"

"We're in something of a stalemate," she said. "Nothing to do with why we were all in Vegas. Just something that…came up."

"Can I be of any help?" Owen asked.

"Nah," she said, unbuckling her seat belt. "But thank you." She wanted to tell Owen everything, but she'd start bawling. And she didn't want to burden him with this right now. He had enough crowding his mind and heart. She also didn't feel right blabbing about Chase's personal business, even if it was hers too.

She gave his hand a reassuring pat. "I'll check in later, okay? You take care of yourself today, Owen."

"I'll try," he said.

She was about to gently remind him to call Tina back, then realized he'd have to anyway in order to pick up Shep and Arlo. That gave her some relief. They'd meet face-to-face, he'd realize how much he liked Tina and they'd be okay again.

She hopped out just as Chase reappeared with her and Danny's bag over his shoulder. It hurt to look at him, so she busied herself by unlatching

Danny from his car seat. Her baby boy was awake and alert, his new little stuffed monkey on his lap.

"I'll haul these up for you," he said. "Be right back," he called to Owen who was moving into the passenger seat.

She gave him something of a smile and led the way upstairs. Once they were in her apartment, he dropped the bag by the door, then gave Danny's head a caress.

"Will you at least think about my proposal?" he asked.

"Nope."

He looked a bit surprised, confused too, then sucked in a breath and nodded before darting out the door and down the stairs.

She closed the door, feeling like she was closing the door on the proposal for good. But as she texted her mom that she and Danny were home safe, she felt those annoying tears pricking the backs of her eyes again.

He proposed, she added. Out of a sense of responsibility.

Three dots appeared, then disappeared, then reappeared. Seconds ticked by, same dots. Finally the text.

Taking rest of day off and will be over within twenty minutes.

Hannah swiped under her eyes and breathed a sigh of relief. Her mother was exactly what she needed right now. And coffee. She had two medium-sized orders to deliver by 6:00 p.m, a no-white-flour-no-refined-sugar-low-glycemic-index dinner for two for the Finchleys, new clients and another pair of newlyweds. The husband was prescribed the new diet, and his bride was joining him in solidarity. They also wanted to hire Hannah to teach them to how to make low-glycemic-index meals. Her other order was a chocolate-swirled cheesecake to celebrate a high school senior's acceptance to her first choice college. All the cooking and baking she had to do would be perfect for today. To take her mind off Chase. And the proposal.

She fed Danny and then held him against her, patting his sweet little back for a burp, then she moved over to the window and just stared out, breathing in the baby shampoo scent she loved so much. Danny's eyes were drooping and it was nap time, so she sang him a lullaby, then another, the one Chase had fumbled the lyrics to in those very early days. But the tears welled again, and her voice started cracking. Danny had fallen asleep anyway. She put him in his bassinet and leaned over to kiss his head.

"Love is everything," she whispered.

Her intercom buzzed, and she pressed the button to let her mom in. Bettina zipped up the stairs, fresh from the bank in her navy pants suit, a bag from the coffee shop dangling from her wrist.

"Tell me everything," her mom said, then pulled her into a hug and kissed her on the cheek. "I brought sustenance," she added, holding up the bag. "Your favorite crumb cake and their very good chocolate croissants."

"Perfect," Hannah said. "I'll make coffee."

"*I'll* make coffee," Bettina said, going into the kitchen. "You sit and talk." She gestured at the table, and Hannah sat down.

Before she'd left for the trip to Las Vegas, Hannah had already told her mom about Kent and the call to Owen from Nevada police. Now she added everything else, starting with Chase making her feel better on the spot about what she'd tell Danny someday, how Chase had accompanied Owen to the coroner's office, the newlyweds in the B&B parking lot and the marriage proposal. That they needed each other, which was certainly true.

"But true *right now*, I think," Hannah said, cutting a slice of the crumb cake as her mother brought over two mugs of coffee and sat down. "Chase only very recently met his father for the first time. He only very recently found out he had an identical twin. That's a lot to deal with and process. And then there's me, a connection to that twin. The mother of his baby nephew. So all this time, we've both been very raw about everything. And then we get the news that Kent died. It's been…a lot. Of course we grabbed on to each other even if I tried really hard to keep my guard up. Of course there's a need for each other *now*."

"How do *you* feel about Chase?" Bettina asked, taking a sip of her coffee. "You like him? You care about him?"

Hannah bit her lip and poked at the crumb cake. "Both those things and…more."

"How much more?"

"I might have fallen madly in love with the guy. Against my judgment and almost my will."

Her mom gave her a gentle smile. "Well, that's kind of how love works. Hard to control. You feel what you feel. And *need* is very powerful. That word might encompass more than Chase realizes."

She wasn't so sure about that. "But isn't all this *need* temporary? We need each other now, sure. What about six months from now when time has helped? When we're both on surer footing. What then? Suddenly we're married and have nothing to talk about."

"This may be your guard talking, Hannah."

"For good reason, though. Do I want a husband

who doesn't love me? No, of course not. You don't want that for me, either."

"That's right, I don't. But Chase wouldn't have proposed if he didn't love you."

Hannah shook her head. She definitely didn't believe that. "He was very clear about why he was proposing. He wants to take care of me and Danny and Owen. Invest in the McCord Ranch to secure Danny's legacy. Give him the family name. He said absolutely nothing about love."

"But don't you think it's love that drove him to all those reasons? That's what I meant by need encompassing more than he realizes. Marriage is a huge commitment. You're a package deal. It's marriage and fatherhood."

"I think he just cares, Mom. That's who he is. He's built of *goodness*."

"I'd get ordained just to marry you two myself," Bettina said—quite seriously.

Hannah's mouth dropped open.

"Because I think he *does* love you. He just hasn't admitted that part to himself because love is what he's so afraid of."

Hannah nibbled on a piece of the crumb cake, trying to find a way to make her mother's theories be enough. But if Chase didn't even know that love was driving him, he certainly wasn't ready to get married. He wasn't ready to be Danny's father.

"Yes, *afraid*," Bettina said. "Think about it, Hannah. It's why Chase never refers to Owen as 'my father.' Chase has been trying to keep Owen out of his heart. To not mourn the separation from his twin—and now the permanent loss. He's afraid and just can't go to those places long shuttered in here," she said, tapping her chest. "So, thanks to that bride, he found a way to make a family with you, Danny and Owen without having to breathe the word *love*. It's too hard for him."

Hannah had gasped at least twice during all that. A lot of that made sense. "But shouldn't he be in a different place before he makes a lifetime commitment to me? To my child? A more settled place where the word *love*, the emotion of love isn't so scary?"

"That's where you come in, if you ask me," Bettina said, biting into her croissant. "He needs you for that. To get there."

"Oh Mom, *pleeeze* stop having an answer for everything that actually sounds right to me," she said only half playfully. "I want him to love me if I'm going to accept a marriage proposal. I need him to love me."

"And you did tell him that?"

Hannah nodded. She reminded her mom what the bride had said—that need was the key to life and to forget all that other crap. Love was included in there. "I told him in very clear words that for me to get married, my husband would need to be in love with me. Love me truly, madly, deeply. I don't think I'm wrong to want that."

Bettina sipped her coffee. "Well, let's see what happens when he has a little time to think. To process your 'no.'"

Last night, he'd seemed more interested in whether a little more time to think had changed *her* answer to yes.

She could see him now, at the ranch, sitting at the desk in the office, Shep and Arlo coming for a visit and a good scratch behind their ears as he stared at the computer screen and paperwork and ledgers. *Was* he thinking about her? Them? Or would he accept her no and that was that?

"He'll be back," Bettina said. "Mark your mama's words."

Her mother was rarely wrong. But Hannah was 100 percent sure that when he did "come back,"— and he would sometime today because he was *staying in her home*—it would be to fine-tune his earlier points and arguments. Not to talk about love.

Forget about declaring it.

Chapter Sixteen

"They do cheer a person up," Owen said as he and Chase stood outside the goat pasture, watching them headbutt and kick around three colorful plastic balls.

Chase rested his forearms on the top of the fence. He'd spent an hour in the office going over the books, then did some physical labor in the barns but the hard work hadn't done a thing for his jumbled mind. The goats were funny, though. "They really do." He glanced at Owen, who looked anything but cheered up. In fact, he looked downright miserable, as though he might actually burst into tears any second. "They should be rented out to anyone feeling down in the dumps. We could make a small fortune."

Owen managed a smile, but it disappeared fast. He was quiet for a few moments, then said, "I guess no matter what, a person just doesn't stop loving their child." His voice cracked on the last two words.

Chase knew Owen had learned that nine months ago, when the truth about Kent had come out. And the pain of it had to have broken his heart all over again with the news of Kent's death.

"You don't have to justify your grief or broken heart," Chase said. "To yourself, first and foremost. Or to anyone else. You're allowed to love Kent."

Owen glanced at Chase. "Hannah said almost exactly that last night when she brought Danny to my room at the B&B. Before whatever happened between you two," he added, a slight question in his voice.

Hannah. The sound of her name had him seeing her beautiful face, long blond hair flowing down her shoulders, her intelligent, fierce hazel-green eyes. He already missed her. And now he had no idea what was going to happen between them. If anything.

"I proposed to her last night," Chase said, surprised he'd come out with it. He hadn't been planning on talking about that at all. "Marriage," he added.

Owen's eyes had widened. He clearly hadn't expected to hear that. "Well, given the silence between you two at breakfast and on the way back home, I presume she didn't say yes."

"My proposal was about how we needed each other. That we should be a family. But she wants her husband to love her, not just need her. I explained that I thought we'd have a great life together. I'd adopt Danny, if she'd allow me to."

"*Do* you love her?" Owen asked.

Chase looked away, out toward the mountains. "I've never been good at applying that word to myself. I know I have strong feelings for her. I have a deep need to take care of her and Danny."

"I'm sure the void in your life where your father was supposed to be contributed to that," Owen said. "Where I was supposed to be."

Chase glanced at Owen, then away. Owen had always seemed okay about talking about this heavy stuff. But it had to be hard on him. It was certainly hard for Chase to *hear*.

"I mean, just like a parent loves a child no matter what," Owen went on, "it's usually the same the other way around. But how does a child love a father who was never there, whose name he didn't even know? The love exists for that child because we're talking about very fundamental issues and relationships, but it gets buried deep and it just goes unused, unapplied. Of course you have trouble with that word, Chase."

Huh. He hadn't expected Owen to understand, let alone to explain what had been a mystery in his own mind, his heart, all his life. Chase had never been able to pinpoint what Owen just had. *Unused. Unapplied.* Buried deep. Still.

"A big piece of me shut down when I walked away from you and your mother," Owen went on. "My wife tried so hard to reach that place inside me, but I couldn't even tell her about leaving you behind as a newborn. How could she ever hope to make me whole when she didn't know the terrible truth? And then when she died, another big chunk of me was gone. Everything left over went to Kent, and I tried my hardest to make up for the deficits. But I guess I failed. I know I did." Owen looked down at the ground, his jaw set hard.

So much of what Owen had just said answered questions Chase hadn't even realized he'd had since arriving in Winston, since learning the truth about his birth.

"You can't blame yourself for Kent's problems," Chase said. "All those what-ifs that I said were helpful in getting me through? They work in any circumstance. Like, what if your parents had offered to take in my mother and me and we all lived together in Winston, and you and Lynne raised the two of us. Brothers. Twins. Who's to say Kent wouldn't have turned out exactly the same?"

Owen gave a miserable shrug. "This is why I haven't called back Tina. All this heavy, depressing stuff is in here," he said, butting the palm of his hand against his head. "And here," he added, slapping his chest. "She doesn't need this."

"She might want it, though," Chase said. "To be there for you. To talk it all over. Or not. You don't have to tell her any of this. You can just let her be there. Just like you'd be there for her if she needed you."

Owen didn't respond, just looked out at the pasture, past the goats. "We're a pair, aren't we," he finally said. "Both of us only able to go so far."

Chase bristled. He did *not* like that comparison. But he couldn't say why. Or that Owen was wrong, exactly.

But then it occurred to him that his less-than marriage proposal wasn't so dissimilar to Owen being unable to return Tina's call. And the woman had his beloved new dogs, for Pete's sake.

"We *are* a pair," Chase said with a heavy sigh.

"Well, that's the thing," Owen said, turning to face him. "The thought of you walking away from Hannah, that beautiful heart and soul, be-

cause of the same bullcrap keeping me from calling back Tina makes me furious. Spitting mad."
He slapped the top of the fence. "I can't stand for
that, Chase. You and Hannah are both pure gold.
And that baby boy—he's the whole world. You
and Hannah belong together."

Chase hadn't seen all that coming. "I could say
the same about you and Tina."

"If I call Tina, will you go tell Hannah you do
love her?"

Chase narrowed his eyes. "That's good black-
mail. Because I do want you to be happy. But it's
not that simple for me." Why was everyone talking about love in this specific case of his? Chase
was a smart guy; he knew that love and marriage
should be one and the same in most relationships.
But he and Hannah had other reasons for marrying. Very good reasons. Chase didn't want to talk
about love or even think about it. It was *need* that
was driving him. And that made sense to him. He
and Hananh truly did need each other.

"And besides, you're not even at the love point,"
Chase pointed out. "You just have to make a *call*.
Apples and oranges here."

"You couldn't be more wrong," Owen said. "I
loved Tina when I broke up with her nine months
ago. And I love her now."

Chase actually gasped. Then he realized that

of course Owen had loved Tina then. It was why he ended their relationship. Because he'd loved her, cared that much.

And he loved her now. But Owen was used to running and hiding when his emotions got to be too much. Pushing away from people instead of bringing them *in*.

Just like Chase had been doing his entire life.

"Well, that's my final offer," Owen went on, a new sparkle in his eye. "I'll call back Tina if you go see Hannah and tell her how you really feel."

One of the goats made a funny sound and head-butted a plastic red ball right at Chase, as if trying to knock some sense into him.

Chase couldn't help a smile forming. Who knew the goats had been listening?

Or that Owen McCord had *wiley* in him?

"I'll go see her, but I'm not sure what will come out of me." And that was the truth.

"It's a start," Owen said, pulling out his phone.

"I'll just head over to Hannah's place, then. You make that call."

Owen tipped his hat and they both walked in opposite directions. Chase turned his head to see Owen with his phone against his ear.

Chase got in his truck and drove toward Main Street, no idea what he was going to say. He only knew he *needed* to see Hannah like he needed to breathe.

But there was that word she didn't like again.

Hannah had just delivered both of tonight's orders when her phone pinged with a text.

Chase.

"Well, he's back," she said to her mom, who had accompanied her on the deliveries so Bettina could watch Danny while Hannah chatted with her new clients and reiterated the instructions for heating and leftovers. They were sitting in the Calhouns' driveway, her mom about to head inside.

"Told you!" Bettina said with a smile.

"Maybe he's here to tell me he's moving in with Owen and that he wants to collect his stuff."

Her mother shook her head. "No way."

Hannah wasn't so sure.

Can we talk? his text read.

Sure. On my way home from dropping off my mom.

Be there in ten.

Hannah held up the phone so her mom could see since the woman was straining to read over her shoulder.

"Call me later, okay?" Bettina said. "And just know everything will be okay. No matter what."

Except for my crushed, stupid heart. My brain that wouldn't listen to me when I said I was staying far, far away from that kind, too good-looking, sexy, wonderful man.

"Thanks for everything today, Mom. You're the best."

"I love you too," Bettina said, dropping a kiss on her cheek before getting out. She went straight to the back windshield in order to wave goodbye to Danny in his rear-facing car seat.

In her apartment, Hannah put Danny in his swing and put on a low lullaby, which helped calm her racing heart.

And waited, goose bumps breaking out on her arms. Just what was Chase going to say?

The intercom buzzed and in moments he was in the doorway, holding a big bouquet of pretty flowers. She wasn't sure what to read from that at all.

"Very thoughtful of you," she said, heading into the kitchen to put the bouquet in a water-filled vase. She set the vase on the table, then turned to him. "So what did you want to talk to me about?"

"Owen said he was going to call Tina. Hopefully they're together right now."

Good. "I'm relieved to hear that. You had a hand in that, I take it?"

He nodded. "In a way."

"Well, however it happened, it's good." She looked at Chase, who seemed pent-up, not relaxed. "Why don't we sit?" She dropped down on a chair, and then he did too.

"I'm obviously bad at this," Chase said. "Explaining myself when it comes to how I feel. In fact, Owen and I had a good talk about exactly that. How we're both bad at that. A pair, he called us."

Hannah smiled. "I've detected similarities in your approaches to women."

"I don't want to get this wrong, Hannah. Not when you're so important to me. And this little guy too," he said, his gaze on Danny in his swing. "I want us to build a life together, be a family."

She tilted her head. "You said that earlier. When you were proposing."

"That's everything, though, isn't it? Being a family? You, me and Danny? Owen too."

She stared at him, understanding him too well. "Oh, so you're square on your relationship with your father?"

She saw him flinch. He couldn't even *use* that word yet. He was not square on anything, not her, not Owen.

"I know I want Owen in my life," he said. "Developing a relationship will take time. Every day is a major step."

"That's fine, Chase. It's great, actually, when it comes to Owen. But if you want to share your life with me, what I need is for you to love me. With all your heart, all your soul, everything you are. If you can tell me you do, my answer is yes."

He stared at her and swallowed, quickly looking down as if to hide it. But she'd caught it. He wasn't here to declare his love. He was here to convince her to say yes anyway.

"I'm sure all that is in our future," he said, his face sort of crinkling as though he was hearing how very wrong that sounded.

Hannah inwardly sighed. "You just said developing a relationship will take time. That can go for us too. I happen to think you're well worth the wait. Of course, I won't wait forever. I mean, if we're a couple for months and you still can't tell me you love me, then…"

"Or we could just get married right now. Tomorrow, even. That's how soon I want for us to be a family. We're just starting at our natural end point. We'd be making a commitment to each other. I'm sure that time will come when I'm… more…" He bit his lip and looked out the window.

This *wasn't* about love for him. And it was becoming more and more clear how much it was about *need* for him. He *needed* to take care of her Danny. "I know you mean well. Very well. But I'd rather start at the beginning and work my way to the end point, the culmination of love and commitment. The marriage you want to start with."

"I just want to give Danny everything," Chase said as if searching for the right thing to say, something that would make his case. "I want to raise him. I want to be his daddy. I want to give him his family name."

"We Calhouns do okay," she said, hopefully not unkindly. "I'm going to tell you something, Chase. I love you. Very much. I love everything you are. I want to spend my life with you. I want you to be Danny's father. I want him to have the family name. But you have to love me back. It's that simple."

"That's simple?" he asked, his blue eyes mirroring the conflict going on inside him.

"It really is. For me. But it's not for you."

He tugged at the collar of his button-down shirt, which wasn't even buttoned up all the way. "I'm… The thing is that… I'm…"

She had to reach deep down to force out her next words. Because what she was about to say was the last thing she wanted. "I think you should stay at the ranch from now on, Chase. On one hand, things feel unsettled between us, fundamentals up in the air. And on the other, it's very settled. We're *not* a pair."

He winced and sucked in a breath.

"You should go now," she said, her voice cracking as she took a hammer to her already broken heart and smashed even the little bits.

She wasn't sure he'd ever break through his own barriers. With her or Owen.

He stood up and walked over to the swing and knelt down in front of Danny. "I'll always be thinking of you, okay?" And with that, he hurried out the door.

Didn't her mother say everything was going to be okay?

Nothing about this was okay.

Chapter Seventeen

Heart heavy and his head ajumble, Chase drove around aimlessly for a good hour, to the point where he'd seen all of Winston, which wasn't much bigger than his tiny hometown of Bear Ridge. He'd passed the elementary school, where Danny would start kindergarten five years from now. He passed the nature preserve, where Hannah once told him she liked to go on thinking walks with Danny. He passed the ranch where the ill-fated auction had been held, when Owen had his panic attack. Then he drove down quiet, dark Main Street and pulled in a spot in front of the diner where it had all begun.

A slip of paper in his mother's possessions had brought him here to Winston. He hadn't even expected to find *information* about his father, let alone have gotten strangely close to him. Or meet the woman he wanted to marry. Or bond with a three-month-old baby. Winston had changed his entire life.

But Hannah's answer was no. For reasons that were true to her, and he had to respect that. He'd stay with Owen for the next few days and then think about heading home to Bear Ridge. His presence would likely be a big help to Owen right now, and Chase would feel good about sticking around, sticking close. He'd invest in the ranch and speed things along there.

And then he'd go.

But he could barely pull out of this spot by the diner where he'd first met Hannah, memories of moment, the talk in the park, the drive to the ranch, their night together hitting him from every angle. He was going to leave town? For good? Buy that ranch in Bear Ridge he'd long been thinking about? Come visit Owen and Danny every major holiday, birthdays?

But if need was the key to life, the reason for getting married, and he couldn't give Hannah what *she* needed, then he had to let her go.

A chill ran up his spine at the thought. How did

any of this make sense? He was missing something. Was he just too far gone? A void unfilled for twenty-eight years was slowly being filled despite Chase's clear resistance to letting Owen in. Was he subconsciously trying to stop that? Was he doing the same with Hannah? He was just trying to do what felt right to him.

Which might be wrong? But how did he follow the wrong road?

Now his head was aching. He lowered the window to breathe in the clean, April air, which had him feeling better, then pulled out of the spot and drove to the ranch, through the gates and parked by the house. He grabbed his overnight bag, slung it over his shoulder and walked up the porch steps. Guess he was staying here after all, when just a week ago the idea had felt like walls closing in on him. That had to be some kind of progress. But Owen didn't feel like a stranger anymore. He didn't feel like his *father*, either, but like Hannah had said, that would take time.

He rang the bell, stiffening a bit when he heard footsteps coming to the door.

He had his back up for absolutely no reason. This was Owen, a good person. The word *father* might be loaded, but Owen was just a person. A person Chase liked.

"Can I bunk with you?" Chase asked when

Owen opened the door, Shep and Arlo sitting at his knees, assessing the newcomer.

"Of course," Owen said, holding open the door wide. "You're always welcome. You stay as long as you want."

"Appreciated," Chase said.

"Hi, Chase," called a female voice from the living room.

He followed the sound. Tina sat in the living room, a fire crackling in the stone fireplace. Two glasses of red wine sat on the coffee table along with a platter of bruschetta and olives. *Well, good for you, Owen*, he thought. Now he felt bad about crashing the romantic setup. He should have realized that Owen and Tina would be together tonight.

"Can I get you a drink?" Owen asked. "Some bruschetta? Tina made it. It's so good."

Tina smiled. "I'll go grab you a plate, Chase."

"That's all right," Chase said. "I couldn't eat a thing right now. It does look good, though. Sorry to barge in and intrude." He nodded at Tina, then turned to Owen as they headed back into the foyer. "I'll get a room somewhere so you'll have privacy. I'm very happy to see Tina here."

"No, don't leave. I'd love for you to stay with me," Owen said.

Chase could see that he'd make Owen feel bad

if he left, and he didn't want to put that on Owen or mess up his reunion with Tina. Chase would stay. At least he wouldn't be interfering with the lovebirds since the master bedroom was on the first floor.

"I take it the conversation with Hannah didn't go your way," Owen whispered.

"Nope."

Owen sighed. "Sorry."

"Yeah, me too," he said. "I'll see you in the morning." He could feel Owen watching him as he headed up the stairs.

On the second floor, he passed the nursery.

He passed Kent's room.

He passed the room Hannah had stayed in the night of Owen's release from the clinic, the one she always stayed in for overnights at the ranch.

He was about to head into the room he'd spent the night in last time, figuring at least it would be familiar. But as he walked in, nothing felt familiar, nothing felt comforting. It was just walls and a bed and a dresser and windows. He left there and went to Hannah's room.

He was probably imagining it, but the room smelled lightly of her perfume. Floral. Pretty. Clean.

He dropped his bag on the floor and then laid

down on the bed, missing her and Danny so much that he felt a new void crater his heart.

Chase hadn't slept well, so when five o'clock shone on his phone screen, he got up. A hot shower helped and now he needed coffee. He went downstairs and found Owen sitting at the kitchen table, a mug of coffee in front of him. Owen was looking out the window but seemed lost in thought.

"Morning," Chase said.

Owen startled and turned. "Help yourself to coffee. Tina brought over some groceries last night—there are bagels and cream cheese, if you're interested."

Chase smiled. "I was very happy to see Tina here."

Owen definitely looked a lot happier than he had yesterday afternoon. "We spent hours talking. I really opened up." He seemed to be prompting Chase to find out if Chase had truly opened up to Hannah.

"Good," Chase said. "I thought I was doing the same but I didn't get very far. Her answer is still no."

Owen frowned. "Neither of you have had the last word. I'm sure of it."

Chase wasn't so sure about that. "Well, I'll definitely start with coffee." He poured himself a mug and added cream and sugar, then sat down at the table. "I've been thinking. I'd like to invest in the ranch. You could buy back some of the land that was sold off. And replace much of the herd. You could use two horses."

Owen looked surprised. "You want to do that?"

Chase nodded. "I believe in this place. And it's my nephew's legacy. It was unfairly taken from you." *Like I was,* he thought, a hard lump forming in his stomach. "I don't have the means to make the McCord Ranch what it was, but I can help get you halfway there."

Because even if I can't feel it, you are my father. And that does mean something.

Chase knew right then that he would leave by the end of the day. Go home. Where he'd have some breathing room from all of this, all of what happened here, these *relationships*.

He was too far gone. Otherwise, things would be different. *He* would be different. But you didn't just change with a snap of your fingers even if you wanted to.

"We can sit down this morning and go over what's needed," Chase said. "And then I'll be heading home."

"You're leaving?" Owen asked. "I was hoping you'd stay. Permanently."

Something shifted inside Chase, something

soft and unfamiliar. He hadn't expected those words, and they meant more than Chase would have thought possible.

"I appreciate knowing that," Chase said. "But I do need to get home."

He'd do some good here with this ranch and leave feeling settled.

"I never expected you to want to invest in the ranch," Owen said. "That means a lot to me."

Chase lifted his coffee mug and so did Owen. They clinked and sipped and then started talking numbers. His shoulders unbunched as personal talk turned to business. An hour and a half later, bagels consumed, Chase and Owen had the future of the McCord Ranch planned. Danny's future.

Then they both spent another hour in the barns, taking care of morning chores, more ideas cropping up for the McCord Ranch, which Chase had noted on his iPad mini. He'd emailed a copy of the plans to Owen, and then finally, they were back in the house for one more cup of coffee.

And now it was time for Chase to go.

Owen's phone rang and he glanced at the screen. "Unfamiliar number." He answered and listened, surprise lighting his face, his eyes widening. "I'll be there. Today at four. Yes, thank you."

Chase raised an eyebrow as Owen put down the phone and stared at it.

"You're not going to believe this," Owen said. "I don't believe it, and I just heard it straight from a lawyer in Mumford, the county seat. Kent's *lawyer.*"

"His lawyer?" Chase repeated. "Surprised and not surprised he had one."

"Apparently Kent left strict instructions that in the event of his death, the lawyer should contact me about his will and estate. The police aren't seizing the estate because their investigation into Kent's schemes revealed how careful he was about how he swindled people. Folks just *gave* him money."

Chase shook his head. He'd read accounts of how difficult it was for people to get their money back, even in lawsuits, from con men.

"According to the lawyer," Owen went on, "Kent left a letter in a safety deposit box detailing who in town gave him how much and wanted me to return that money. He also noted that there should be enough left to get the ranch back in business. He also left a letter for me, one for Hannah and one for 'The Baby.' Oh—and he'd paid back what he owned on his gambling debts, so no one will be coming after us on that end."

"Wow," Chase said. "I'm beyond speechless."

"Same." Owen shook his head in wonder. "The shocks just keep coming."

"When did he write that will and the letters?" Chase asked. "Did the lawyer say?"

Owen nodded. "Back in December. So four months ago."

"Christmas season. Maybe that meant something to Kent."

"He always liked Christmas," Owen said. "I guess he stockpiled his money and figured if something happened to him, he'd make sure it went back to those it really belonged to." He took a deep breath. "I do wonder what those letters say."

Chase was curious too. He imagined they'd be short and sweet. An *I'm sorry*. "Sounds like he was trying to make things right, in his own way. He took that redemption journey after all."

Owen brightened at that. "It does seem that way, doesn't it?"

"I'd like to invest in the ranch all the same," Chase said. "To be a part of it. But you can make that call." *Now that you don't need my capital.*

Owen smiled. "I'm glad. You're a McCord too," he added, taking a sheepish glance at Chase. "If that's all right."

"I am a McCord," Chase said slowly. Because he was. DNA said so. He just had no idea if he'd ever be able to embrace being a McCord in any-thing other than name only.

And he could leave Winston more fully know-ing that Hannah and Danny and Owen would all be okay. The news didn't take away from all that happened, but it would help the healing process. Hannah and Owen had both been stuck for the past nine months. Now, they could truly move on.

"I assume you won't leave without saying good-bye to Hannah and Danny," Owen said "You'll tell her about the call from the lawyer?" he asked. "She and I need to be at his office at four for the reading of the will and to sign whatever papers."

"I'll tell her," Chase said. "I'll be heading out now, so I'll stop over."

Owen sighed heavily. "I hope you'll be back, Chase. I sure hope so."

If this were a movie, Chase would pull Owen into a hug and then leave. But it was his life in-stead, and everything was coming at him so hard and fast that he all he could do was gulp down the rest of his coffee.

Hannah had just put Danny down for his nap when her phone rang.

Chase.

"Can I come up?" he asked. "I have some news. A lot of news, actually."

Good news? Bad news? He sounded so neutral.

"Sure," she said, her heart starting to pound.

Calm down, she told herself. Just hear what he has to say. "News" was a strange way to put *I've come to tell you I do love you.* So it was definitely not that.

Then what?

She waited by the intercom. In moments he buzzed and she pressed him in, then opened the door.

He came bounding up, wearing a dark green Henley and faded jeans and work boots. Why did he have to look so good?

Before she even had the door closed behind him, he told her about the call Owen had received from Kent's lawyer.

"What a huge relief!" she said, hand to her heart. "My parents. Jasmine and Michael. Countless others. They're all getting their money back. And it means we have a more definite answer for Danny. His father *did* try to redeem himself—in ways he could, anyway—in the end." Her eyes filled with tears. "Danny will have peace in his head and heart about it. That's everything, Chase."

Chase nodded and seemed too emotional to speak. He came farther into the apartment and sat down on the sofa.

Peace when it came to unsettled—and unsettling—family matters *was* everything. Hopefully it would seep into Chase's body and do some good.

"And he left a letter for Danny?" Hannah said, sitting down beside him. "I think that's good. Very good. That'll mean something to Danny when he's older."

Chase nodded. "I feel like I'm saying goodbye with all of you in a good place," he said—tightly.

Hannah frowned. "Good place? My heart is *broken*, Chase. You do know that, right? It's not your fault. You didn't break it—I did by getting involved with you. I told myself to keep my distance, but I just couldn't. Love won. And I lost."

He squeezed his eyes shut for a moment. "I'm sorry I hurt you. You know that's the last thing I wanted."

"I know," she said. And she did know it. It just didn't help.

"Can I say goodbye to Danny?" he asked.

"Of course. I guess you should pack up the rest of your things before that."

He nodded and quickly did, then she followed him to the doorway of her bedroom and watched as he went to the bassinet and dropped a soft kiss on Danny's head.

"I'll be back for your first birthday," Chase said. He ran a hand over Danny's hair and then sucked in a breath before quickly heading toward the door. Hannah led the way back to the foyer.

How she wasn't in a puddle of tears on the floor she didn't know. But she was determined to hold it together. She owed Chase a lot. She was mad as hell at him, but the aching heart had the anger on the back burner.

How could he leave? How could he walk away from them?

You do *love us, I think. I felt your love. Why can't you?*

She knew it was for the same reason he couldn't feel Owen as his father. He had a concrete wall up. And she hadn't been able to chip it, let alone blast through.

He squeezed her hand as he had a million times since he'd arrived in Winston and then opened the door and practically ran down the stairs.

Then he was back up in a flash, pulled her into his arms and said, "Bye, Hannah."

And was gone again.

To stop herself from bursting into tears, she grabbed her phone and texted her mother the news, then Jasmine. About the lawyer and the reading of the will at four, how she was 99 percent sure they'd get their money back. She added to Jasmine that she'd totally understand if Jasmine wanted to go bigger with her wedding plans. But

Jasmine wrote back that she loved her wedding plans as they were, including her caterer—but she was definitely hiring a real photographer instead of her "fumble-fingers" cousin.

Her mother texted: I said it once (literally) and I'll say again: he'll be back. And long before Danny's birthday.

Now the tears did come. *I don't know, Mom*, she thought. But that ever hopeful part of her lived on.

Chapter Eighteen

Like last night, Chase had ended up driving around Winston, unable to actually drive out of the town. *Yet*, he figured. In his state of mind, which wasn't good, he couldn't imagine hitting the road. He'd left Hannah's apartment over two hours ago. He'd found himself driving over to the nature preserve and walking around for a while. Then went to the park where he and Hannah had had that first cup of coffee together. Then he drove past her building three times, just needing to be near where she was.

He was trying to figure where to go next when he realized he'd left his new iPad mini in the barn at the McCord Ranch this morning. There. He had an immediate destination. He'd get his iPad. He'd take one last look at the McCord Ranch, say goodbye to the goats, to Shep and Arlo, if they were outside, and then he'd leave again.

Maybe he'd feel less numb the second time. How he could feel so numb when he missed Hannah so much was beyond him. Maybe he'd found a way to get a handle on his feelings for her.

When he arrived at the ranch, he saw Hannah's little car parked by the barn. His heart leaped and he wondered where she was. Cleaning out the stalls? Showing Danny the goats?

No—because he caught a glimpse of her far off in the distance, walking toward the mountain, her back to him, with Shep and Arlo padding ahead of her. She had on a straw hat, her long blond hair flowing behind her.

He wanted to run after her, throw his arms around her. But she'd made herself clear, and he couldn't give her what she wanted.

Go get your stupid iPad. Say goodbye to the goats. And then go since that is your plan. Just go already.

Something glinting in the sunshine caught his attention to the left of the barn, inside the goat enclosure by their log. Something coming out of the ground. A horizontal sign with words carved into it. Chase stepped closer to see it.

The Lynne Dawson Memorial Farm.

He was so surprised, so touched, that his hand flew to his mouth. Owen must have been working on the carving for days, ever since they'd talked about his mother always wanting a dairy farm. The two goats were headbutting their balls, one flying up in the air and hitting Chase right in the head again.

He chuckled. "Oh yeah?" He tossed the ball back, his gaze on the sign.

You'd like that, Mom. I know you would.

He'd call Owen from the road and tell him he saw it and thank him.

He was about to slip through the half-opened double barn doors to get his iPad when he heard Owen's voice. He stopped, staying just outside in case Owen was in there with Tina, and Chase didn't want to interrupt anything.

"Your mama and I will be going to Mumford in a little while," Owen was saying. Clearly to Danny. He peered in and saw Owen with the baby in his arms, standing in the goat pen but looking out the window, which was slightly open to let in the gorgeous April breeze. "Things are going to be okay. In one regard, I suppose. But we're gonna be hurting here for a while now that Chase is gone.

Your uncle Chase is something special, Danny. But you'll know him your whole life because he'll be there for you. I have no doubt of that."

Chase bit his lip. He should go back to his truck, give Owen his privacy. This wasn't meant for his ears. But he couldn't make himself move.

"I wish I could tell Chase how much I loved him his whole life, every day of his life. I loved him when he was a tiny newborn, and it broke my heart in two when I had to say goodbye to him. But I never stopped loving him. Never stopped thinking of him. He was my son every day of my life, even though we weren't together."

Chase swallowed against the lump in his throat.

"I wish I'd told him all this when he was here," Owen continued, "but I think it would have sent him running for the hills. Though I suppose he did go running anyway."

Chase froze. He *was* running away. He hadn't thought of it that way. He had met his father. He had helped turn things around here. He had helped give Hannah back her trust in people. In men.

And then…ran from her.

His shoulder muscles tensed, as they always seemed to these days.

"It's okay, though, Danny," Owen said. "I believe the bonds are there but this relationship will take time and it's worth every minute. I wish I could tell him how proud I am to be his father, but I don't know if I have that right."

Tears misted Chase's eyes and he blinked them back. This was his father.

My father.

He felt something give way in the center of his chest, and without thinking about it, he just walked right into the barn. "You do have that right," Chase said.

Owen's head whipped around. He couldn't look more surprised.

"What I didn't realize until this moment," Chase began, "listening to all you just said, was how proud I am to be your son. I think I was running from *that*. All that *feeling*."

Tears dripped down Owen's face. He wiggled a hand from around Danny to swipe at them.

"And all that feeling also sent you running from Hannah," Owen said.

Because I love her, he realized, the truth slamming into his head. Into his heart, which ached with just how much he did love her. And he'd been about to run away from it for exactly the reasons his father said.

His father. Not just *Owen.*

Father.

"You might not think you're capable of love, Chase, but I know you are. I see how you are with

Hannah. And with Danny," he added, ruffling the baby's hair.

"And with you, Dad," Chase said, hearing his voice crack. It cracked like the hard shell around his chest, crumbling into dust.

Owen gasped. "I'd give you a full-on bear hug, but we'd squish this little guy."

"I do love Hannah," Chase said. "So much I think I'll burst with it."

"Go tell her," Owen said. "She's taking a walk up north of here to clear her head before the big meeting at the laywer's. Just follow the gravel path and you'll see her."

He knew he'd never forget this moment. The moment his father sent him after the woman he loved. Not just needed—loved. To make a family whole.

Right now, Chase felt *everything*. He just hoped he wasn't too late.

Hannah supposed she should turn back. In an hour, she and Owen were due at the lawyer's office. Once they were done there and walked out and came back home, it would be a true fresh start. The past would be settled. And the present wouldn't have Chase in it. Right now, she needed to keep the in-between going for as long she could.

She just wasn't ready to face that present and future without him.

She wondered where on the road Chase was now. Halfway home, probably.

How she wished this could have been his home. This *was* his home. He just didn't know it.

She lifted her face to the sun, her heart heavy and hurting. She couldn't stop thinking about Chase. To the point that she was hearing his voice, calling her name.

"Woof. Woof-woof!"

Shep and Arlo had turned and were running back toward the barn. She turned, a figure in the distance coming toward her.

Calling her name. She hadn't imagined it.

"Hannah."

She froze, using her hand as a shield from the sun. Chase.

He was running toward her.

The dogs caught up with him and he gave them each a pat, then kept walking until he was right in front of her.

He was here. Not on the road. He was right here.

"I do need you, Hannah Calhoun. But I also love you. With everything I am. I love you. So much."

Hannah gasped. She wanted to pinch her arm to make sure this wasn't a dream.

"I want to marry you because I love you," he

continued. "And because you love me. And because I want to be Danny's father. I'm done running. I'm *home*."

She flung herself into his arms, and he kissed her and then swung her around, getting another set of *woofs* from the dogs.

And then as they held hands and walked back toward the barn, he told her all about eavesdropping on Owen's conversation with Danny in the barn. About his mother's memorial sign. About how his heart had cracked wide open with all his father had said. Yes, *his father*.

Thank God for overheard conversations with three-month-olds, she thought. You could say things to a baby you might not be able to say to anyone.

"Welcome home," Hannah said.

Epilogue

It was the event of the year in tiny Winston, Wyoming, a double September wedding at the McCord Ranch, and it seemed like most of the town had come to celebrate the marriages of Hannah and Chase, and Owen and Tina. Tina had actually trained Arlo and Shep to each carry a little padded tray with the rings down the aisle. Of course, they had to be part of the ceremony.

Ever since Jasmine's wedding back in June, the McCord Ranch had become quite the venue for ceremonies and events. The stables were full of horses again, the pastures and ridges chockfull od cattle. And the Lynne Dawson Memorial

Farm was a petting zoo where local schools came on field trips.

Chase and his father waited at the end of the aisle, a red carpet runner all that stood between him and his bride, who he could see stepping from behind the makeshift tent where she and Tina had been getting ready, attended by their mothers and matrons of honor, Jasmine and Tina's best friend Eleanor.

Chase sucked in a breath as the wedding march began and his beautiful bride came down the aisle, her father's arm around hers, Tina and her father beside them. Hannah looked like a movie star in a long satiny white gown with beading at the waist. A veil covered her face but he could still see her.

And then she was at his side, holding his hand.

He'd never been so ready for anything than to say "I do" to this woman.

That day he'd come to his senses in the barn, he'd accompanied his father and Hannah to the lawyer's office, and they'd all been stunned by the letters Kent had left for them—and Danny. They were short, but full of apology. To Danny he'd written, *To my baby: You made me want to be a better person.—Your father, Kent McCord.*

Hannah had burst out crying.

So had Owen.

Chase had held Danny in his arms, grateful.

Sometimes, everything made sense, and in that moment, everything had.

They'd come home to the ranch and a celebration dinner that Hannah had whipped up. Owen had invited Tina, and he'd stunned them all by returning from the patio with Tina "to look at the stars" with an engagement ring on her finger. Then they'd spent the rest of the evening making plans for the future. Hannah and Chase would build a house on the ranch with a view of the spectacular mountains, and Tina would move into the main house with Owen. Shep and Arlo could come and go from both homes.

Chase would adopt Danny and make him an official McCord. After twenty-eight years, the groom would take his father's name—Chase Dawson McCord—as would the bride, Hannah Calhoun McCord.

And the McCords would take back their legacy and begin again.

* * * * *

Look for the next Dawson Family Ranch book,
Seven Birthday Wishes,
Coming in July 2023!

And in the meantime,
try these other great western romances from
Harlequin Special Edition:

Valentines for the Rancher
By Kathy Douglass

Their Texas Christmas Match
By Cathy Gillen Thacker

The Cowgirl and the Country M.D.
By Catherine Mann

Available now!

#2965 FOR THE RANCHER'S BABY
Men of the West • by Stella Bagwell

Maggie Malone traveled to Stone Creek Ranch to celebrate her best friend's wedding—not fall in love herself! But ranch foreman Cordell Hollister is too charming and handsome to resist! When their fling ends with a pregnancy, will a marriage of convenience be enough for the besotted bride-to-be?

#2966 HOMETOWN REUNION
Bravo Family Ties • by Christine Rimmer

Sixteen years ago, Hunter Bartley left town to seek fame and fortune. Now the TV star is back, eager to reconnect with the woman he left behind...and the love he could never forget. But can JoBeth Bravo trust love a second time when she won't leave and he can never stay?

#2967 WINNING HER FORTUNE
The Fortunes of Texas: Hitting the Jackpot • by Heatherly Bell

Alana Searle's plan for one last hurrah before her secret pregnancy is exposed has gone awry! Her winning bachelor-auction date is *not* with one of the straitlaced Maloney brothers but with bad boy Cooper Fortune Maloney himself. What if her unexpected valentine is daddy material after all?

#2968 THE LAWMAN'S SURPRISE
Top Dog Dude Ranch • by Catherine Mann

Charlotte Pace is already overwhelmed with her massive landscaping job and caring for her teenage brother. Having Sheriff Declan Winslow's baby is just *too much*! But Declan isn't ready to let the stubborn, independent beauty forget their fling...nor the future they could have together.

#2969 SECOND TAKE AT LOVE
Small Town Secrets • by Nina Crespo

Widow Myles Alexander wants to renovate and sell his late wife's farmhouse—not be the subject of a Hollywood documentary. But down-to-earth director Holland Ainsley evokes long-buried feelings, and soon he questions everything he thought love could be. Until drama follows her to town, threatening to ruin everything...

#2970 THE BEST MAN'S PROBLEM
The Navarros • by Sera Taíno

Rafael Navarro thrives on routines and control. Until his sister recruits him to help best man Etienne Galois with her upcoming nuptials. Spontaneous and adventurous, Etienne seems custom-made to trigger Rafi's annoyance...and attraction. Can he face his surfacing feelings before their wedding partnership ends in disaster?

HSECNM0123

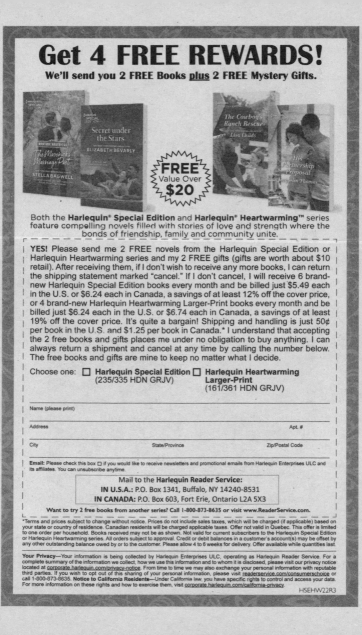

Get 4 FREE REWARDS!

We'll send you 2 FREE Books plus 2 FREE Mystery Gifts.

FREE Value Over **$20**

Both the **Harlequin® Special Edition** and **Harlequin® Heartwarming™** series feature compelling novels filled with stories of love and strength where the bonds of friendship, family and community unite.

YES! Please send me 2 FREE novels from the Harlequin Special Edition or Harlequin Heartwarming series and my 2 FREE gifts (gifts are worth about $10 retail). After receiving them, if I don't wish to receive any more books, I can return the shipping statement marked "cancel." If I don't cancel, I will receive 6 brand-new Harlequin Special Edition books every month and be billed just $5.49 each in the U.S. or $6.24 each in Canada, a savings of at least 12% off the cover price, or 4 brand-new Harlequin Heartwarming Larger-Print books every month and be billed just $6.24 each in the U.S. or $6.74 each in Canada, a savings of at least 19% off the cover price. It's quite a bargain! Shipping and handling is just 50¢ per book in the U.S. and $1.25 per book in Canada.* I understand that accepting the 2 free books and gifts places me under no obligation to buy anything. I can always return a shipment and cancel at any time by calling the number below. The free books and gifts are mine to keep no matter what I decide.

Choose one: ☐ **Harlequin Special Edition**
(235/335 HDN GRJV)
☐ **Harlequin Heartwarming**
Larger-Print
(161/361 HDN GRJV)

Name (please print)

Address   Apt. #

City   State/Province   Zip/Postal Code

Email: Please check this box ☐ if you would like to receive newsletters and promotional emails from Harlequin Enterprises ULC and its affiliates. You can unsubscribe anytime.

Mail to the **Harlequin Reader Service:**
IN U.S.A.: P.O. Box 1341, Buffalo, NY 14240-8531
IN CANADA: P.O. Box 603, Fort Erie, Ontario L2A 5X3

Want to try 2 free books from another series? Call 1-800-873-8635 or visit www.ReaderService.com.

*Terms and prices subject to change without notice. Prices do not include sales taxes, which will be charged (if applicable) based on your state or country of residence. Canadian residents will be charged applicable taxes. Offer not valid in Quebec. This offer is limited to one order per household. Books received may not be as shown. Not valid for current subscribers to the Harlequin Special Edition or Harlequin Heartwarming series. All orders subject to approval. Credit or debit balances in a customer's account(s) may be offset by any other outstanding balance owed by or to the customer. Please allow 4 to 6 weeks for delivery. Offer available while quantities last.

Your Privacy—Your information is being collected by Harlequin Enterprises ULC, operating as Harlequin Reader Service. For a complete summary of the information we collect, how we use this information and to whom it is disclosed, please visit our privacy notice located at corporate.harlequin.com/privacy-notice. From time to time we may also exchange your personal information with reputable third parties. If you wish to opt out of this sharing of your personal information, please visit readerservice.com/consumerschoice or call 1-800-873-8635. **Notice to California Residents**—Under California law, you have specific rights to control and access your data. For more information on these rights and how to exercise them, visit corporate.harlequin.com/california-privacy.

HSEHW22R3

HARLEQUIN PLUS

Try the best multimedia subscription service for romance readers like you!

Read, Watch and Play.

Experience the easiest way to get the romance content you crave.

Start your **FREE TRIAL** at
<u>www.harlequinplus.com/freetrial</u>.